W9-BNP-136
Bathsheba,
Bathed in Grace

How 8 Scandalous Women
Changed the World

Carol Cook

WestBow
PRESS
A DIVISION OF THOMAS NELSON

ISBN: 978-1-4497-7266-6 (sc)
ISBN: 978-1-4497-7267-3 (hc)
ISBN: 978-1-4497-7265-9 (e)

WestBow Press books may be ordered through booksellers or by contacting:

WestBow Press
A Division of Thomas Nelson
1663 Liberty Drive
Bloomington, IN 47403
www.westbowpress.com
1-(866) 928-1240

Library of Congress Control Number: 2012919869

Printed in the United States of America

WestBow Press rev. date: 1/8/2013

ENDORSEMENTS

There are many books about women of the Bible, but ***Bathsheba Bathed in Grace, How 8 Scandalous Women Changed the World***, has to be at the top of the list. It is unusual in style and insight – for once, a totally relatable recounting of Biblical history shared in a manner anyone can identify with and benefit from. It puts flesh on the bones of real women of the Bible and does so in a way that fills in the blanks. As a counselor, it makes sense to what might have truly happened. You will want to read this page-turner. I highly recommend it to everyone.

Rev. Alfred H Ells, Author, Church Consultant, MC., Executive Director-Leaders that Last Ministries

In her new book, Carol Cook takes us on a journey back in time to walk in the footsteps of eight exceptional women of the Bible. Faced with seemingly impossible situations, we watch them find courage, wisdom, and grace through prayer and faith. These ancient stories continue to hold meaning and provide women of today with sources of inspiration as we seek to navigate our complicated world.

Susan Polman, Author: Half Way to Each Other

Scripture comes alive when you can identify with the struggles of ordinary imperfect women and their stories as beautifully written by Carol Cook in Bathsheba: Bathed in Grace. You will find yourself on these pages and be challenged to obey God's call on your life. Like Hagar, one of these Biblical women, you will know that you are also seen by God. Don't miss this incredible read that will challenge you to change your world. ***Carol Travilla, M.A. Lifeplan Facilitator and Spiritual Director, Author: Caring Without Wearing, Co-Author: The Intentional Woman***

Bathsheba: Bathed in Grace is a profoundly poetic retelling of the Biblical stories of women who changed their worlds as they basked in the reality of God's forgiveness and grace. You will be entranced by their lives and the profound application to your own life, as I was for mine! Truly, a 'Holy-Page-Turner' of God's goodness to those He loves! ***Naomi Rhode, CSP. CPAE Speaker Hall of Fame, Past President National Speakers Association, Past President Global Speakers Federation, Co-Founder SmartPractice***

Carol Cook's book feels as though we are invited inside the private homes of eight women of the Bible. As they open their door to welcome us in, we step into the pages of the Bible that reveal how they have decorated our lives with the choices they have made. As we take a tour though their stories, we begin to recognize how much we have in common. Together, we sit down in a comfortable place and begin to share...chapter by chapter; we find that these biblical women share our joy, our pain, our temptations, our fears, our hopes, and most of all our questions to God about the whys in our lives. ***Carlette Patterson, Sports Life-Coach, and Author: I Thought We Had Forever***

Carol Cook's collection of Bible stories told from the perspectives of the women who lived them is bold, original, and unpredictable. Carol's narratives bring these women of old—whose trials and transgressions are often painfully close to home—right into the present day. One can't help but be drawn into their riveting tales as this well-researched book informs, instructs and entertains. ***Tammy LeRoy, Author/Editor of seven books, including "Along the Cowboy Trail"***

The problems and challenges of yesterday and today blend in this imaginative retelling of eight age-old stories about Bible women. Their lives parallel the contemporary issues we are experiencing on the front lines with women today. ***Holly DelHousaye, Executive Director, Center for Women with Vision, Phoenix Seminary***

Foreword

Our friend Rachel can teach you about the futility of bitter emotions, Leah will explain how unrealistic pressures affect our lives and Sarah knows all about the illusion of control. No, these are not wise women in our current coffee klatch, but rather the historic biblical heroines whose stories inform the way we live.

From Eve to Hagar, the trials and triumphs of powerful feminine figures in scripture help us learn from every experience. These timeless tales are a testament to God's infinite understanding of our lives and they are as relevant to today's reader as they were when the Holy Spirit inspired their telling so many years ago.

Proverbs 31:26 reads, "She opens her mouth with wisdom and the teaching of kindness is on her tongue." This describes the spirit of Carol Cook's God-guided book Bathsheba: Bathed in Grace (How 8 Scandalous Women Changed the World.) Turn the first page and lose yourself in stories of remarkable women who will change the way you view your own personal history and how you will shape your limitless future.

Sara O'Meara

Sara O'Meara

Childhelp Chairman & CEO

Yvonne Fedderson

Yvonne Fedderson

Childhelp President

Introduction

TWENTY-FIVE YEARS AGO, I found myself an empty nester with a growing sense that I was alone in my daily journey. Our three children were off to college, my husband Jim, focused on his burgeoning business, and I was...empty. Life had led me into a new and unfamiliar season, and I searched for meaning.

I sought many cures for what ailed me, all the while struggling with long held issues of unforgiveness, perfection, control, unrealistic expectations, and simply feeling invisible much of the time. These issues were not new—they had been forty-two years in the making. But having had three children in five years, the daily bustle of child raising and homemaking kept these obstacles conveniently buried, That is, until I found myself alone.

Clawing my way through insecurities, lack of accomplishments, and no real intent or purpose, I discovered that I could find solace in serving others. This led to many charitable opportunities and the chance to meet hundreds of other women whom I grew to admire for their ability to hold down jobs, raise families, and still fit in the time to serve others. In fact, when I stopped focusing on my own situation, I grew to love the life I was living "outside" myself.

I remembered the New Testament saying that the older women should serve the younger, and I realized this was the new season I had entered into—I was now an older woman! Eventually, I was drawn to help, teach, and mentor young women, and I began guiding personal Bible Studies directed toward them. We read through the books of the Bible and reflected on the life God intends for his beloved children.

Years led to a decade, and after many book studies, my friend Carlette approached me and said she believed I was to write the next Bible study that would begin in the fall of that year—a character study of women in the Bible. Looking at all the patriarchs first, we soon wondered if there were enough women mentioned in the Bible to do a full course of study. Research revealed at least 418 women who were named!

I never imagined so many examples of women were hidden in the pages of God's word. I became fixated on knowing more about these women. As I read their stories—some only a few sentences long—I recognized many of the same struggles I had faced on my journey to know God more intimately. I wrote first about the woman caught in adultery. I felt her pain. I asked her to share what it was like being caught in the very act, dragged out, half dressed, to face a public forum of judges. The punishment for such a crime was stoning. What a horrible way to die. And where on earth was the man she was caught with? Somehow, I saw him sneaking out the window and slinking away.

Of course, all of this was prearranged by those who wanted to challenge Jesus, so they could bring her before Him. As a result, she was able to partake of His Divine forgiveness and set her tarnished life on a positive path. Through this story, it became clear that I should take up my Bible, read other women's stories, and share them in first person—letting each woman share her own story from her own perspective. Once I was set on this course, the stories would not stop playing in my head. The ladies talked non-stop telling me their stories from their own point of view. Eventually, each found her unique voice.

I spent many hours researching the Bible, commentaries, and other books. It became my quest to find every book I could on what had been written about these women. I built up my library and consumed the viewpoints and opinions of each author. Originally, I intended to write only about New Testament women since I had rarely read the Old Testament… it seemed too hard. But soon, I was drawn to start at the beginning with Eve and tell it all—from Eden to Bathsheba to Lydia and the Women of Philippi.

To put myself in their shoes, I dressed up as the Bible women as I wrote about them, and I had photos of each on the wall of my office along with maps and timelines of each era. Soon, I had written the narratives of twenty-four Bible women. After making the decision to write their stories in book form, I opted to divide them into three books. In this book, eight special women share the issues, power, and purposes of their lives: Eve, Sarah, Hagar, Rebekah, Leah, Rachel, Tamar, and Bathsheba.

I found myself living inside each woman as she struggled in her life, and came to relate with her pain, joy, and situations I had experienced in my own life. The day I determined to publish the work, it was as if, like Sarah, I was going to give birth to a child in my old age! To share my thoughts and emotions about the women who have been my sisters gave me Holy insights into God and His intention for my own life.

It is my hope that this book will help any woman who feels trapped in the circumstances of her own story to move ahead and leave behind the baggage of the past. My prayer for each reader is that she will learn to accept her imperfections, allow God to restore her soul, and begin to refine her own story with new insights gained from the stories He has shared with us of these legendary women of the Bible.

Acknowledgements

I OWE MY DEEPEST debt of gratitude to the Holy Bible. It's timeless account of Biblical stories woven throughout centuries as encouragement, warnings, and lessons to learn…

To Jim. My teacher, mentor, encourager, I am indebted for eternity. Your prevailing love carried me to new heights as I overcame the fear of getting personal with Bible women. They came to life, enhanced by your vivid recollection. You have read the Bible over and over and hold each story dear. Early morning lattes and devotions together spurned me on to believe in myself and this work. Our partnership was made in Heaven and soon to be half a century. I thank you.

To my children and grandchildren, you helped me hold onto my dream of making this book a reality. Bryan, Theresa, Creed, my soulful champions, I am grateful. To Carlette, you knew I had this book within me before I did. To Fran for the beautiful cover and staying with me on the journey. To Sandy, for lunches and lattes over titles, covers, and content.

To my endorsers, you read the stories and trusted belief that hope could be endowed to the readers. Bless you. To all the women who sat through classes where I spoke in each character voice to you throughout a whole year…your encouragement carried me.

To my energetic and effervescent editor Karen Ball, who believed in me and caught my vision—I owe much. Knowing scripture and the characters as you do, kept me on track and on purpose. Thank you.

To all the writers of books on Bible women, I pray blessing and favor to you.

Table of Contents

CHAPTER 1
Bathsheba

I SIGHED, OPENED THE narrow door leading out onto my roof, and pressed my bare feet on the first stone step. With each familiar footfall, I embraced the serene moment. How many times had I completed this holy sacrament in the years of my womanhood? The cleansing ritual I would observe here tonight. Too many to count.

Unlike the day since I said good-bye to Uriah. I could count each one of those days. Every one made my heart ache.

I knelt as Tzipporah, my nursemaid since childhood, poured cleansing, warm water over my hair. As she dried the heavy tresses, for they had never been shorn and fell below my waist, I welcomed the first of the restoring tasks I would perform tonight.

Even now, Tzipporah anticipated my every need. She knew I preferred to finish bathing in solitude, so stood and, almost before I noticed, departed.

My peaceful roof. I came often to this sanctuary to meditate, renew, and restore. My healing place waited now, offering its warm balm to soothe me.

In the twilight, the stars reminded me of God's light and favor. Darkness would soon descend, making the moon appear brighter still.

My monthly cycle of nidah was finished, and the mandatory seven clean days passed. This ceremonial cleansing signified purity that I was now prepared to have relations with my husband...but he was away.

I took in the verdant beauty around me. Saffron and wild thistle thrived in pots on the terrace. Flax plants—soon to be woven into linen, cords, and ropes—stirred in the gentle breeze, inviting me.

The tenderness of the late spring evening enfolded me, like a warm fire on a cold winter's day.

By next month, the ivy and fragrant blossoms of passion vine would fill in and block the latticework around me, eliminating outside distractions, and making me invisible here in my perfect cocoon.

I followed the row of lit candles casting a radiant glow over the space, and dropped my azure linen robe as I sat on the limestone bench. I pulled the pins that held my hair, and the ebony locks that Uriah loved so well fell around my shoulders and down my back like a delicate curtain. I stroked the long strands until they surrendered to the rhythm of my ivory brush.

Thus prepared, I turned to the footed copper-and-stone tub. How it welcomed me, reminding me, in its strength and perfection, of Uriah's arms about me. Such generosity and love shown when he purchased this magnificent bathing vessel for me. As a child, I knew what it was to be cherished. My father and grandfather treated me as something treasured. It amazed me yet that one such as Uriah treated me like a lamb from his flock—not just a lamb in his field, but one brought into his home, doted upon....

Beloved.

Uriah, my noble and decorated hero warrior, was in battle with all the Kings Men of Israel, struggling to conquer the fortified city of Ammon, near the Dead Sea. So far removed from me.

I picked up the oil of myrrh, which came from the presses of En-Gedi. I let it flow into my palm, then rubbed my hands together, cupped them to my face, and inhaled. The musky scent permeated the air and floated above me, teasing my senses. I massaged the oil into my hair, letting the strands play through my fingers. Even in the moonlight, I saw the sheen the oil imparted.

I stepped into the mikvah and sank into the intoxicating mix of coconut milk, rose petals, and oil. The liquid, warmed by the afternoon sun, enveloped me.

If only my beloved Uriah were here tonight, but as a renowned warrior in the Army of Israel, he slept not in our grand bed, but on the ground in an open field near his enemies. Silence pierced my space, like an unwelcome visitor. Loneliness fell upon me.

"I miss you, Uriah."

I could almost hear him say, "I miss you too, my love."

I was blessed.

Sweet slumber beckoned, but there was another element of my ritual to complete, so I turned my heart to my evening prayer and blessing. "Adonai Elohai—blessed are You, LORD, our God, King of the universe, who has sanctified us with Your commandments and have commanded us concerning immersion. Make me pure and clean tonight, both in body and soul. LORD God, protect Uriah. For he is not safe, as I am here at home. Yet he is safe… in Your arms."

My eyes drifted shut and I sank into the stillness of God's presence. I knew He had heard me and would answ—

What was that?

I bolted upright, and clutched my arms to my chest. I sensed something in the night around me. Something…invasive.

Was someone there? I snatched my robe and slipped into its protective covering. Something was wrong. I felt…I felt….

Someone's eyes on me!

I abandoned my bath and hurried to the safety inside. But as I reached the door, I glanced back over my shoulder…past the roof…past the homes around me…

To the palace above.

There on the king's balcony, a shadowy figure!

I hastened inside, away from prying eyes. Who could it have been? Surely not a soldier…a sentinel on his rounds? No, he would not stare. To take his eyes from his assigned task would mean certain death.

I sat at my dressing table, clutching the robe at my throat. To feel this way in my own home, as though something had been taken from me!

I tried to secure my hair with pins but my trembling hands would not cooperate. I pressed them on the dressing table and spoke words of comfort to the face in the bronze mirror. My breathing slowed. I drew a deep breath and looked into the reflected eyes before me.

"This will not happen." I steadied my voice. "No shadow in the night will rob me of my safety in my own home."

Enough. I would fear no more. Rather, I would dress for my evening meal. Tzipporah had labored long preparing my favorite meal of hummus, flat bread, and olive tapenade. I would not disappoint her. I would dress and partake of her gift.

No sooner had I lifted the gown that awaited me than a loud knock sounded on my door. I turned. "Who is there?"

"Messengers from the palace."

Why would I receive a message from the palace of the king while Uriah was away at war? Never had this happened in my years here in Jerusalem. "Yes?" I tried to keep my voice steady.

"You have been summoned to the palace."

The calm I fought so hard to regain melted away. For the king to summon me...and to do so at night...I fought imagining what event would necessitate my presence at the palace—and lost.

Uriah! Had he fallen on the battlefield?

Oh no, not this, not now...My heart raced and I was unable to think clearly. I could not bear losing Uriah. Or, was it my father? They were among David's Mighty Men, The Thirty, whom the king trusted above all. What tragedy had visited these I loved to bring royal messengers to my door?

"Adonai, help me." I clasped my cold, clammy hands together but my body radiated heat. Confused signals sparked in my brain, but didn't guide me to what I should do....

Must get dressed...must go....

Again, I started toward the bed for the comfortable gown Tzipporah laid out for my evening at home. No, no, this will not do for a visit to the royal palace. To honor Uriah tonight, I needed something noble and regal...from my beautiful clothes...must look my best to honor Uriah....

I rushed to ready myself. I parted the drapery with a harsh movement of my hand and pushed it back to reveal my lovely gowns and formal attire. I must find the perfect ensemble...I needed Tzipporah. I could hardly catch my breath, let alone make such an important decision.

"My Lady," the messenger's voice raised a notch. "We must hurry."

"I will come straight away."

I grabbed the fabric in front of me as clothes fell to the floor in disarray. My eyes locked on the scarlet gown I had yet to wear. Perfect. I slipped into it and adjusted the sash. I replaced my hairpins with jeweled combs, laced my sandals, and took a pashmina wrap for my shoulders.

I hurried from my dressing room and made my way to the entry. Oh, if only Tzipporah were here to receive the news with me. News for which I was not prepared...would never be prepared. Whatever my loss, she would help me stand strong. Yes. I must stand strong.

I opened the door half way, as if to soften the delivery, and looked into the eyes of two men, the king's sentinels. My voice trembled. "What has happened?"

"Happened? This we do not know."

A summons from the king was not a royal invitation, but a direct order. There was no choice. I knew I must go at once. I closed the door behind me and left the shelter of my home.

The awkward silence begged me to fill in the blanks. I walked between my escorts trying to keep up with their pace. I dared another question. "Has something happened to Uriah?"

"We have no information. Only that your presence is required at the palace tonight."

"Who requires my presence?"

"The king, of course."

I frowned. "So, the king is home and not on the battlefield?" My question went unanswered. I shivered in spite of the warm night air, pondering with each step. What would I do if Uriah had died? Or Papa wounded, or my grandfather, the king's political advisor—dead? Of course, because these men were beloved confidants of the king, he would want to tell me himself, in person.

The shopkeepers were preparing to close their souks. Soon they would make their way home. I was struck that regardless of this invasion of my world, that my life was about to change in a tragic way, their lives continued all around me as just another day in the city of Jerusalem.

As we approached the palace, I looked up to behold the mighty fortress in its majestic splendor. Torches cast a burnished glow on the guards. The sentinels called, "Open on orders of the king." I couldn't help noticing the bronze lion crest in the middle, which boasted an enormous gold D that reflected the moonlight.

David, the Lion of Judah.

The lion wore a crown— the root of David had triumphed. Somehow, this symbol left me with a sense of dread for I knew not what was to be revealed inside those gates.

We moved though the courtyard and gardens that graced The Royal Palace. We ascended the wide marble steps with stone lion statues mounted on either side and entered through enormous carved doors. Down the long corridor of mosaic tiles we moved by the light of the ornate bronze candelabras.

This visit was in stark contrast to previous ones. The king's warriors and their wives often gathered in the grand reception room for feasts and banquets, celebrating the many victorious battles. On those visits, I'd taken careful note of every detail, of the walls lined with burgundy drapery on iron rods, embellished with ropes and tassels that cascaded effortlessly in a puddle on the floor. Of the ornate decorations, the lush furnishings, the detailed murals. Everything was palatial and fitting for a king.

This time, though I was closer to it all than ever before, I scarcely noticed. I had eyes only for our destination.

At last, we were there, The Throne Room. The doors opened and there he stood.

King David.

The guards escorted me forward. They bowed and started to move to each side of the throne, but David stopped them with his raised right hand. "Leave us."

I was struck by the man's direct gaze and my breath caught in my throat. The champion, standing tall and military straight, one who had subdued the most powerful armies and thrived in all his endeavors, strong with authority emanating from his very presence. Was it any wonder the people choose him for their king? I should be honored that he invited me here for this news.

Instead, I was terrified. And yet...

He didn't have the look of loss on his face, as I'd expected. No sorrow weighed his features or gaze. I tried to anticipate by his demeanor what news awaited me, but I discerned nothing.

"Have you taken your evening meal?"

His question startled me. My evening meal? What did food matter at a time like this. Still, he was the king, and I had to respond. I nodded, my gaze drifting to the marble tabletop near the throne. My eyes rested on two gold chalices that stood there, then came back to him. He moved down the steps with athletic grace and went to recline on a leather couch, which boasted one arm and pillows of goats' hair as bolsters. He made a sweeping motion for me to follow suit. I took my place on the wood-framed scarlet couch. It matched my gown.

"Join me with a cup of wine, Bathsheba."

The king had the manner of a welcoming host and not that of a bearer of bad news. "Yes, My Lord." It might help settle my nerves.

He indicated a silver-footed tray bearing pomegranates, roasted nuts, figs, and dates. In the center stood enormous silver candle stands topped with candles, which cast a crimson glow. The wax ran its course onto the grapes and dripped on the tapestry without concern or care.

"I am not hungry My Lord. I desperately want to know why I am beckoned here. I fear the worst but I am prepared to receive the devastating news you have for me."

"Devastating news?"

"Yes, Lord."

He stood and came to sit by me on the couch. "Bathsheba, I have no devastating news for you. You are here only because I desire you."

His words pierced my heart. So…this summons was not about the safety of Uriah or my family at all. It was about me!

The king was wrong. This news *was* devastating. I was not to lose my husband…but my honor.

"I saw you bathing through the lattice work on your terrace."

It was the king?

"In my Kingdom, Bathsheba, there is no one who compares to your beauty. I determined I must and would have you this very night."

How could this happen? "Please, Lord, no. I belong to another and you… you may have any woman in your kingdom. Though I have given Uriah no children, he desires only me. My husband could have taken other wives, could have fathered children with them. But he wanted none but me."

For a moment, the room fell silent. Then David stood and extended his hand. I met his eyes and at that moment, I knew. Like a hawk caught in the net of a fowler, I knew.

My fate was sealed.

I stood and placed my hand in the king's outstretched hand.

Forgive me, Uriah.

I waited to hear David's deep breathing and slipped out of his presence, careful not to awaken him. I focused on getting to the door without making a sound, and then pulling it closed behind me. I must go to my home.

Back through the courtyard, I trudged. My hair fell across my face and mixed with the tears I tried to control. The guards opened the gates, staring straight ahead. I was invisible. The same gates that led me to the king now closed me out, leaving me in my shame. I turned to see the Lion of Judah crest again. I had come through these gates at my husband's side so often, celebrating victory. Now they mocked my disgrace.

The Lion, my king, had devoured my life.

Beyond the glow of the palace gates, I made my way home. Alone. It was dark on the street where I lived and for this, I was grateful.

At my courtyard, I stood frozen, gazing at my door. How everything had changed. My heart forbade me to enter, to bring my shame into my sanctuary. Exhausted, I slumped on the cold stone bench under the myrtle tree in the garden. The flowers had just started to bloom. I had used them for my chuppah canopy on my wedding day.

My head hurt, but not as much as my heart. The smell of lilies captivated the air, leaving a pure and innocent scent, a fragrance I used to love but now detested, for I was neither.

It was then that a terrible truth pierced me. I was no longer Uriah's pure and beloved lamb. I had been sacrificed on the altar of the king's desire.

"God, help me."

I knew not how long I stayed in the garden before I stood to unlatch the door. I searched for a candle, lit it, and placed it by my bed.

How I longed to be cleansed, but dared not go back to the roof. I stared at my dressing table, where my gaze fell on the shears. A madness grew within me, urging me to seize them and cut away at my hair even as the king had cut away at my life. But to do so would destroy what Uriah loved. Had the king not done enough of that for one night?

I turned and grasped the linens on my bed and collapsed beneath them. My mind thrashed. Was I to blame? But how could I be? I had followed the law. I had bathed at twilight for my purification, as was the custom. How could such obedience lead to dishonor? I had done nothing wrong.

I missed Uriah so much, but now I dreaded his homecoming. If he knew the secrets of this night, death and devastation would be ushered forth like a raging beast, devouring its prey. Either my warrior husband would kill the king, or be killed himself in the attempt.

But wasn't death what I deserved? The Jewish Law called my stoning. What, then, were my options? Tell Uriah, tell my family, or claim rape. But no, my only safety was silence.

My decision was made. I would stuff all the ugliness and deny it to surface ever again.

And so the days passed and yet against my will, the secret shamed my every waking thought.

Finally, one morning, Tzipporah looked at me with a questioning eye. She knew something was eating away at me like leprosy. "Are you ill, My Lady?"

"I am fine. I just miss Uriah."

She looked into my eyes, as she had so often when I was a child, to see if I was hiding something—and I most certainly was. Although I trusted her with my life, and I longed to share my shame, I could not. For it would put her at risk as well.

She stayed close the next weeks and offered her silent comfort. Her small frame was beginning to show signs of age, but such beauty rose from her servant heart. Never far from me.

"Anything you need, My Lady…just ask."

I attempted to resume my life. I pretended for weeks that everything was all right, but I was unable to escape the darkness that so judged me. All food and drink sickened me.

Tzipporah made flat bread, matzo soup, and herbal tea but nothing helped. Her heart ached to the rhythm of my own. I needed her near but pushed her away. I could not be comforted. I could neither sleep nor eat.

The nausea grew like a tidal wave until one morning its waters pounded upon my reluctant soul. I couldn't lift my head from the pillow…and I knew.

My fear increased tenfold as my monthly cycle passed without evidence. Tzipporah was as worried as I've ever seen. She kept my schedule and so knew at last what tormented me. Still, she didn't speak of it.

I was pregnant—with King David's child.

Terror replaced the shame that hovered over me. Secrecy could no longer be my covering. My secret was about to be shattered like an alabaster jar, never to be restored.

I sat at the table for the better part of the day—a blank parchment and inkwell stalking me. At last, I lifted the pen and wrote four words across the page: "I am with child."

I rolled the scroll tight and sealed it with the wax seal, House of Uriah, and sent Tzipporah to deliver it. "Quickly now, see to it that this message gets to the king—and the king only!"

I expected a response before nightfall, but I waited for days to no answer or acknowledgement from the palace. So, it was as I suspected, the king cared not for me or the torment smothering me. I waited and worried. Every day brought me closer to judgment, although inside I was already condemned. With no defender, I would tarnish my family's and Uriah's good name, finishing my days as "Bathsheba the harlot."

Then, finally, messengers arrived at my door but the news they bore brought no relief but further devastation: "Uriah the Hittite has died bravely in battle."

I fell to my knees, face down on the cold floor, and wailed out my sorrow. Tzipporah came running.

"My Lady, My Lady! What is it?"

Nothing she said could comfort me. I would by no means be comforted, not now, not ever.

I had lost my beloved. Never again would he embrace, touch, or hold me. Grief took up residence within and was redefined as I mourned. I questioned God, and prayed to die. To join Uriah in death would liberate me from my shame and my raging secret.

Perhaps death was my answer.

But no. One who took his own life was buried in a desolate cemetery outside the city gates. Family and friends were not allowed to mourn this death. I couldn't commit yet another sin.

Even as I wept, I was not sure if the tears were for Uriah or for me. There was more than a baby growing inside. Consumed on one hand by my secret, grieving my many losses on the other, the future held no hope.

Outwardly, I mourned the compulsory period, yet inside mourning would be my companion all my days. I would gladly wear the widow's clothes forever, that is, if…I survived the secret.

"My Lady, there are messengers at the door."

I turned to Tzipporah. What now? What more could be taken from me?

I went to the door and found not just a messenger, but the king's attendants as well. So then, was I to be taken and stoned? I held my hand out to the messenger, who laid a scroll in my palm. I broke the royal seal, opened it, and read.

Come to the palace and become my wife.

The words slashed me like a lightning bolt across the sky. My trembling fingers nearly dropped the parchment on which King David had penned the words. He could have me now that I was without a husband. He could have taken me as his concubine, diminishing my standing but saving my life. But no, he chose to marry me. My king's decision would redeem both my baby's life and mine.

For this, if nothing else, I was grateful.

One of the attendants spoke. "My Lady, The king asked us to escort you to his palace."

"I will be but a moment." I stepped back inside and looked around my familiar rooms, and beheld the treasures of my life here with Uriah. I chose a few: The hairbrush my grandmother gave me when I was a little girl and the Blue Nile pearls from my mother. I picked up the shiny gold bracelet—a present from my father when I had become "a woman." I touched it to my lips, and slipped it on my wrist.

I brought my favorite gift from Uriah: the polished, filigreed bronze mirror on a pedestal that he had taken from the plunder of the Philistine camp. I gazed at my reflection. How my life had changed since I said good-bye to him in the spring, never imagining it would be my final farewell.

I handed the treasures to Tzipporah and she bound them together in her basket and prepared to go with me.

I breathed a silent good-bye, dismissing the dreams that were not to be. I glanced at the wedding bed Uriah had carved for us from the Cedars of Lebanon. Sweet memories of his deep faith and his immeasurable sense of honor and justice hovered here. He amassed great wealth from military conquests and divided the spoils among his men. His fortune would well keep the staff here and cover the expenses of caring for his home.

I exhaled. This chapter was over and another beginning.

Together, Tzipporah and I departed. We followed the attendants to the City of David. I didn't know whether to love or hate David for his intrusion into my life. I would revisit this issue another day.

As I approached the palace, I couldn't help reliving my last visit. Today, I was not invisible. The shofar blew upon my entrance. Tambourines played along with lyres, harps, and flutes. Had David written the music for this occasion?

To my surprise, the king stood, awaiting me, just inside the gates. It was an awkward moment. He stepped close and kissed both my cheeks. "Welcome to your new home." I could not read his features, could not tell what emotions lay behind those eyes. But for now, it was enough that I had husband, a father for my child, and a covering.

There was a special suite prepared for me near David's chamber. "Do not worry; you will always have access to me."

I did not know if this was a good thing or not.

My palace life was one of privilege as I experienced favor over all the other wives. David meant what he said about providing for me. I became a public figure, taking on a queen-like role in the palace because of David's preference. He astonished me by asking my opinion on court matters. But what surprised me most was my growing contentment here in my new surroundings.

Though the other wives may have suspected my baby would come early, no one mentioned it and the remainder of my pregnancy passed without incident. The morning sickness stopped and I marveled seeing David counting the days.

So many days he looked at me and said, "Perhaps today I will hold my child."

"Perhaps."

"I am overcome with joy to hold him and bless him on my knee."

"Soon, David."

When my delivery came, the midwives attended me, and when they laid my child on my chest, told me, "You have given the king a son." In that moment, I felt what I never thought I would feel again—joy. My son would be handsome and strong, just like his father.

In this blessed moment, I drifted into sweet slumber. I awakened to see David holding our sweet boy on his knee, with his hand on his tiny head. The blessing he longed to give…now received.

Hours later, I sat in the nursery gazing out the window as I cradled my son. I was surprised to see Nathan, the prophet, in the inner court. We were not expecting him to come so quickly. Nathan, the court historian, temple musician, and trusted advisor, came often to bring encouragement and give the Word of the Lord to David. Elohim spoke directly to him. He was the messenger, and David the student. By now, Nathan was our faithful friend who would perform the ceremonial rites at the baby's circumcision and naming service in eight days. But since he was here now, I knew David would want me to bring his son to meet Nathan.

I rose and started for the courtyard. As I approached, I heard Nathan speaking, but his words were not those of congratulation and so, I stopped. I clutched the child to me as I listened. This was not the voice of a friend! This was the voice of a Prophet of the Lord God.

Oddly enough, Nathan was telling a story.

"There were two men in a certain town. One was rich, and one was poor. The rich man owned many sheep and cattle. The poor man owned nothing but a little lamb he had worked hard to buy. He raised that little lamb, and it grew up with his children. It ate from the man's own plate and drank from his cup. He cuddled it in his arms like a baby daughter. One day a guest arrived at the home of the rich man. But instead of killing a lamb from his own flocks for food, he took the poor man's lamb, killed it, and served it to his guest.

When David spoke, fury burned in his heated words. "As surely as the Lord lives, any man who would do such a thing deserves to die! He must repay four lambs to the poor man for the one he stole and for having no pity."

Nathan's next words took my breath away. "You are that man. The Lord God of Israel says, 'I anointed you king of Israel and saved you from the power of Saul. I gave you his house and his wives and the kingdoms of Israel and Judah. And if that had not been enough, I would have given you much, much more. Why then have you despised the Word of the Lord and done this horrible deed? For you have murdered Uriah and stolen his wife. From this time on, the sword will be a constant threat to your family, for you have despised me by taking Uriah's wife to be your own.'"

So, the prophet knew my shame!

"I have sinned against the Lord."

I had never heard such sorrow in David's voice. In any man's voice. Nor had I ever heard such compassion as was in Nathan's next words.

"Yes, but the Lord has forgiven you, and you won't die for this sin. But you have given the enemies of the Lord great opportunity to despise and blaspheme Him, so…your child will die."

The moment he finished speaking, the baby started in my arms. I stood frozen, unable to believe what I had just heard. It could not be true! It couldn't. It took a moment to realize heat radiated against me. I looked at my baby.

He was burning hot against my cold body.

Court physicians and men of prayer were summonsed. I called for Tzipporah.

David begged God to spare the child. He went without food and lay all night on the bare ground. The leaders of the nation pleaded with him to get up and eat with them, but he refused. They had never seen their warrior king so distraught and repentant. He tore his clothes and groaned, "God help me, hear my prayer. O God of my Fathers, have mercy!"

David's lament resonated through the palace, down the halls, and through the walls.

Like an earthquake reshapes the surface of the earth and alters the course of rivers, affecting lives and destinies, so forceful were the events of that one night, of the decisions the king made. My world, my future, and my reality were altered forever through no choice of my own. With one obsession, the courses of life, death, and a nation's destiny were rewritten, and the most powerful king on earth was brought to his knees.

As was I.

I placed the fevered child in Tzipporah's arms and for the second time in a matter of months, I fell face down on the terrace floor. Was not this the wrath of God against David? Must I be punished as well? "Adonai, I don't understand...Please, help me."

Feeble and powerless in my own grief, still trying to process David's confession, I sat by our baby's bed, cradled him to my bosom, and rocked back and forth to the rhythm of his unsteady heartbeat. Since no name would be given until the circumcision ceremony, Yeshoua—Joshua, became my name for him until that day.

I could feel no compassion for David, nor could I comfort him. As if struck mute, I was unable to speak or think clearly. Numbness had taken residence inside me.

I had lost Uriah, might lose my only child, and was not sure I wanted to have David, either. I watched the king lie on the cold, stone floor while I held my little prince. As long as I held him in my arms, he might not die.

Yet, in the wee hours of the morning, on the seventh day, I watched Yeshoua surrender and take his last breath. Our beautiful boy, born out of this traumatic and volatile union, was gone from me. I laid him on the magnificent brass bed. I turned to my attendants.

"Go tell the king, 'Your son is dead.'"

I died too. Death was all around me. My life was ebbing away, one tragedy at a time.

David would have no use for me now, nor I for him. "Why was I not the one to die?" Or David? Why did he not die instead of my innocent baby. To live in this imposing edifice could never make up for the loss of my child.

One moment I felt like a victim and the next a villain for the distain I felt for David. Feeling sorry did not help because I lived in constant memory of the wrong to which I had been a party. Unwilling yes, but still, I kept thinking…

If only.

Weeks later Tzipporah came to my chamber. She opened her arms wide and reached for me. I welcomed her embrace.

I closed my eyes. "How fares the king?"

"The king mourns no more, for the moment your son died…he got up, bathed, changed clothes, and went to worship in the Tabernacle of God. The king asked the servants to bring food. They were astonished. But he told them, 'As long as the baby was alive, I held out hope but when he died, I knew I couldn't bring him back, but someday, I can go to him.'"

"Thank you, Tzipporah."

"Of course, My Lady, anything at all."

One afternoon, David came into my room. I wanted to turn from him, pull the covers over me, but something within urged, so I sat up.

"Bathsheba, may I sit?" He paused, as if needing my permission. I nodded.

"I have missed your presence in the palace. I longed to see you and bring comfort to you. Though our child has gone to rest in the arms of God, I know you weep and mourn still." He paused as if making sure the words perched on his lips were right.

"I wrote a psalm that calmed my anxious and weary soul when I was running from Saul, hiding in the caves of En-Gedi, and engaging in many fierce and dangerous battles."

"Yes, Lord,"

"The Lord is my shepherd, I shall not want. He makes me to lie down in green pastures; He leads me beside still waters. He restores my soul…"

The silence melted away as I began to weep from the depths of my soul, with guttural groans and sounds I could scarcely believe were coming from me. My sense of feeling returned and I was moved. I knew my need.

I turned to my king. Held out my arms.

"Bathsheba."

I leaned in to him and surrendered my heavy yoke upon his shoulder. He raised his strong hand and pressed my head more firmly to him. I yielded to his tender care.

Inside my soul, Adonai began cutting away the bitterness and unforgiveness I harbored for so long. I stayed with the pain until it was done. David continued to hold me as I drifted off, halfway between reality and slumber.

"He…restores my soul…He…" The words played in my head long after David uttered them. I knew God wanted to restore my soul. I needed His restoration. I was ready for my healing.

Something was stirring again. I could stay locked in the prison of my pain forever, or I could forgive David, thus freeing us both.

I had felt dead for so long…I took a deep breath. "LORD God, forgive me and grant me courage to start over."

I sat back and looked into David's eyes. "I forgive you." I straightened as I realized the words were true and inside, it was I who was now freed.

Able to begin anew. I saw that I was not the only one to lose a child. "Oh David, I am so sorry your son died."

He exhaled deeply, took my hands, closed his eyes—and wept. I leaned into him and in that moment, our hearts fused. Everything had been said and words were an intrusion.

Welcome blessed, healing silence.

I dedicated myself to the man who now held my wounded heart in his strong and steady hands. Though much had been done to me, I was grateful for new beginnings. This decision caused an enormous transformation. God was indeed restoring my soul.

As David comforted me in the months ahead, I experienced a new life with him, with a new script, after such heartbreak, doing things out of love was a balm of warm ointment covering my soul.

Finally the day came when I gave the king news I knew he'd longed to hear. "We are going to have another child."

David took me into his arms. "God is too good to me."

"That is His nature, My Lord."

"Still…"

We named our son, Solomon—Peace.

David's life had been about war, fighting, and hostilities but this son would bring peace to Israel. Through this child, God restored us. The weight of sin had felt unbearable but understanding forgiveness, even in our wrong choices, taught me a lesson I never forgot: forgive, forgive, forgive.

It seemed David and I were the only ones living in the palace but there were the first wives and concubines living there too. Although the women had private chambers, we met communally and I interacted with them during the day as the children played their hero games: Philistines vs. Hebrews, Gideon vs. Midianites, but mostly, they reenacted David and Goliath, each crying "My turn to be David the shepherd boy."

We chatted about life, daily activities, and our children's intellect, talent, and strength. Fierce competition grew among the boys and I discovered each mother had plans for her son to become the next king.

As did I.

David and I had four sons, and I relished being the last wife he chose. After Solomon, we named our next Nathan, for the beloved prophet. He tutored our boys in music, Israelite history, and most importantly, the ways of the Lord. Shobab was born next, and we rejoiced for the Lord's blessing. I conceived again and bore a son we named Shammua.

The king was at last content and God gave him rest…from all his enemies.

One day David came to me. "Bathsheba, I want Solomon to sit on my throne and reign as King of Israel after me." Though our son was not the king's eldest, I held on to that promise and hid it in my heart.

The king's health began to decline and he lost strength every day. He talked again of building the Temple of the Lord in Jerusalem. It was his last passion before dying. "How can I live in this magnificent palace of wood and stone when the Lord God is dwelling in a tent in the wilderness? I must build a temple for Adonai Elohai Yisrael."

Since the time Moses and the Children of Israel wandered in the desert, the Ark of the Covenant of the Lord had passed from city to city, and now the king brought it to Jerusalem. The Tabernacle Tent was just beyond the palace walls.

I encouraged David to call Nathan and ask him to consult with God about this burning desire.

Nathan went before the Lord and then returned to us. "God spoke, 'Say this to my servant David, You are not to build a house for my Name, because you have shed much blood on the earth in my sight. But you will have a son who will be a man of peace and rest, and I will give him rest from all his enemies on every side. His name will be Solomon, and I will grant Israel peace and quiet during his reign. He is the one who will build a house for my Name.'"

Another confirmation.

My heart wanted to cry because of the death of my king's dream. I could see David was disappointed, but I knew he was glad that his son would be able to do this for his God.

"So be it." David's acceptance was clear in his tone.

"God said to tell you He will always be with you, but because He called you to be a man of war and not a man of peace…" Nathan waited, for David was ready to speak.

"It is because of all the victorious battles God gave me?"

"Yes."

"Eighty-five wars in all."

"He knows."

With a renewed passion, David drew the exquisite plans for the temple as the Spirit of God directed him. He had amassed a fortune for use in the temple construction.

He appeared before all the people one last time to tell them of the great plans. Then he told Solomon, in the presence of all his kingdom, "And you, Solomon my son, take heed now, for the Lord hath chosen you to build a house for the sanctuary. Be strong, and do it."

"Thank you my father, May God reward you for your service."

"He already has."

My king grew closer to death.

Nathan the prophet arrived and came to me, I was surprised at his coming to me first, until I heard the news that made me heartsick. Adonijah, the king's eldest living son, had proclaimed himself king that very day, making sacrifices. What's more, he had followers—among them, the king's general Joab, all the king's sons, and Abiathar the priest. Neither Solomon nor Nathan were invited.

Nathan's eyes burned. "The king must know immediately. Go and tell him this news, Bathsheba. After you enter, I will come in and remind the king of what he told you regarding Solomon and of what God told him."

I entered the king's room and bowed before him.

"What do you want Bathsheba?"

I stood. "My Lord King, today your son Adonijah has attempted to seize the throne and appointed himself king. You gave me your solemn promise that our son Solomon would sit on your throne."

Nathan entered, so I bowed again and started out the door as Nathan began to speak.

"Have you, My Lord the King, declared that Adonijah shall be king after you, and that he will sit on your throne? Today he has gone down and sacrificed great numbers of cattle, fattened calves, and sheep. He has invited all the king's sons, the commanders of the army and Abiathar the priest."

Disgust burned within me as I left the room. Solomon was the rightful heir to the throne, and his family would be killed immediately by the person trying to steal the position of the throne. I would die as well. How could Adonijah betray not only his dying father, but his king as well? To usurp the kingdom and overrule God's plans for his people. How could he?

I leaned against the wall just outside the doorway, breathless as I listened.

Nathan's voice rang out. "Right now they are eating and drinking and saying, 'Long live King Adonijah!' But I, your servant, Zadok the priest, Benaiah, and your son Solomon he did not invite. Has My Lord the King done something without letting me know who should sit on the throne after him?"

I tensed, waiting for David's response.

"Call in Bathsheba."

I started. He was calling for me? The attendants came to the door and escorted me in.

The king sat up and when he spoke, his voice resounded as vibrant and strong as ever. "As surely as the Lord lives, who has delivered me from all my trouble, I will carry out this very day what I swore to you by the Lord, the God of Israel. Solomon your son shall be king after me, and he will sit on my throne in my place."

My heart stopped, almost letting me forget to bow. I fell on my face before the king I had grown to love and accept. "May My Lord King David live forever!"

David had saved my life and my baby's life before by taking me as his wife. And now he had saved my life and my son's life today! Gratitude welled up like a spring as I rose up with renewed hope for the future. "Adonai."

I stood back and waited, for I had not been dismissed. The king turned to his servants. "Call in Zadok the Priest, Nathan the Prophet, and Benaiah."

They arrived and bowed in unison.

"Take Your Lord's servants with you and have Solomon my son mount my own mule and take him down to Gihon. There have Zadok the Priest and Nathan the Prophet anoint him as King over Israel. Blow the trumpet and shout, 'Long live King Solomon!' Then go up with him, and bring him to sit on my throne and reign in my place. I have appointed him ruler over Israel and Judah."

They answered the king, "Amen! May the Lord God so declare it."

So they left with Solomon to do all King David commanded.

I was in the garden, reliving David's words, when I heard the loud sound of the trumpet, followed by shouts from the city, "Long live King Solomon!"

I heard the crowds rejoicing as their praises resounded up the hill, so loud the very earth shook beneath me!

God had prevailed.

It was done.

Nathan returned with news that Adonijah and Joab heard the trumpet and the people rejoicing. When told about Solomon, Adonijah so feared for his life that when he felt the earth move, he ran to the Tabernacle of the Lord to cling to the Horns of the Altar, a symbol of refuge and protection. His older brother Absalom had died when he tried to overthrow the kingdom. He must have feared.

Had he known the same fear I had this morning when I heard his news from Nathan? A new king often killed all those in line for the throne, except his own sons. Had Adonijah's plans to seize the throne been successful, certain death would surely have befallen both Solomon and me, perhaps before the sun went down. Now....

What would King Solomon do to him? Would he show mercy or seek revenge? I remembered David telling Solomon to be careful about General Joab and others in the kingdom.

At the end of our meal, Solomon rose, called for his guards, and ordered them to bring Adonijah.

He came and bowed down to King Solomon. The king, my son, looked at his brother. "I have pardoned you. See to it that you show yourself worthy. Go to your home."

And yet, even as I watched the defeated usurper leave, something told me this was not the last time Adonijah would try to steal the throne.

Walking to David's room, I was pleased to give him the blessed news.

"My Lord, as you so commanded, tonight Solomon sits on the throne of Israel in your place."

He looked up from his bed and waved his hand. I smiled, comforted that David's kingdom had passed into anointed and blessed hands, and my life had been saved.

I sat by the king's bedside during his last days. We discussed our life together and acknowledged that he was close to death but soon would be privileged to hold our precious son already in Heaven… again.

"Bathsheba…book of my Psalms."

"Yes, Lord."

I brought it. He could no longer see clearly. I opened the faded and worn parchment on which he had penned his poetry, hymns, prayers, and thanksgiving. It opened to a creased place…and I read:

"Yea, though I walk through the valley of the shadow of death, I will fear no evil, for thou art with me. Thy rod and thy staff they comfort me. Thou preparest a table before me in the presence of mine enemies; thou annointest my head with oil: my cup runneth over. Surely, goodness and mercy shall follow me all the days of my life, and I shall dwell in the House of the Lord forever."

I looked up to see his lips form the word, "Amen."

Tears flowed down David's weathered face. He raised his seventy-year-old hands upward. I felt the presence of the Almighty in the room attending him as his soul soared peacefully, like a bird returning to his nest in the heavens. My king walked through the valley of the shadow of death, arriving peacefully into the arms of God, his Father.

David, the man who had never lost a battle, was victorious even now in death, his last battle, and came to rest as, "The man after God's own heart."

I closed his eyes—and wept.

In my youth, I thought David would always be with me. I had given thirty years of my life to him, and they passed like vapor through the air on a windy day. It was not enough.

I thought of his mission in the later years of his life, how after his great sin he vowed, "Bathsheba, I want to finish well." And he surely did. He ruled the Kingdom of Israel for forty years, and all the people loved their mighty warrior and king.

Since kings of the day had many wives, there had been no queen sitting in the palace in Jerusalem. Solomon invited me to sit in his court. I agreed—the second time I had said yes to a king. I cherished being the first Queen Mother of all Israel. I had the ear of a king once again and was able to influence political and social events in the court.

King Solomon had two magnificent marble thrones built and seated me in the place of honor at his right hand.

Like his father before him, he took to writing. One book he called the Proverbs of Solomon, in which he penned the adages of old, many that I taught him and his brothers from their youth.

Using the pseudonym name for King Solomon, "King Lemuel," he dedicated the last proverb, number thirty-one, "The Virtuous Woman" to me, referencing the power of living a surrendered and productive life.

He wrote the Songs of Solomon and penned the book of Ecclesiastes. One of my favorite readings was in Ecclesiastes 3. He called it, "A Time for Everything."

> *"There is a time for everything, and a season for every activity under the heavens: a time to be born and a time to die, a time to plant and a time to uproot, a time to kill and a time to heal, a time to tear down and a time to build, a time to weep and a time to laugh, a time to mourn and a time to dance, a time to scatter stones and a time to gather them, a time to embrace and a time to refrain from embracing, a time to search and a time to give up, a time to keep and a time to throw away, a time to tear and a time to mend, a time to be silent and a time to speak, a time to love and a time to hate, a time for war and a time for peace."*

In my lifetime, I lived all these seasons and learned lessons in each. As I forgave and trusted David, I was led to trust God and grow to a life beyond imagining.

I owned the secrets in my life, knowing God already knew. He…who knew my past, present and future—was with me. Forgave me. Restored me. Out of the ashes of my life, when I had lost all hope, God brought hope, honor.

Once surrendered, I never gave up trusting God.

And He never stopped blessing me.

Read Bathsheba's Story in 2 Samuel 11-12, 1 Kings 1

Chapter 2

Sarah

I **LIFTED THE CURTAIN** flap of the tent. Another hot, almost unbearable day in Canaan. I took note of my once beautiful flowers, now bent over, and browned by the scorching mid-day heat. Everywhere I looked…our land was dried and parched.

When Abram brought me here five years ago, it was lush and beautiful. What had happened to my lovely home…the Promised Land? I wrung my hands, but the sights around me told me more than I wanted to know. Where was Abram? Where was his God? Had my husband gone to his altar to seek wisdom from his Holy One?

I feared what news might be given him by his God. I do not fully understand the Lord God of my husband. I do not know that even He can save this barren, desolate place we have called home for so many years.

I saw Abram coming. His hurried pace and drawn face did not bode well. Alarmed, I rushed to greet him. Something was wrong. He stepped inside our tent, breathless. "Sarai, I have run out of options for us." He paused, as though selecting his words carefully. "If we are to survive this famine, we must leave our home and go to Egypt, it is our only hope. There we will have an abundance of water, food, and pastures."

I looked fully into his eyes, seeking any hope of resistance. He was adamant. Words failed me. My fear gave way to all this change would bring to our world. When we came here, my husband said our journey was complete and at last, this would be my home forever. Yahweh God had told him. But, could I survive a journey to another foreign country?

How could I?

"Sarai, I know this is not the news you longed for, that you hoped for a sign of rainstorms from the east, but it is not to be. If we stay here, we will perish. I will not let that happen to you and our families. I commanded Eliezer to prepare everyone and everything. We shall move out in two days."

We. That meant everyone. Every man, woman and child, along with all the livestock, possessions, and whatever meager provisions we had left. No trace would linger.

My heart broke. Our last hope had evaporated with the moisture in the ground. A severe dust storm blew over Canaan today mocking us as tumbleweeds propelled across the desert. Abram prayed for rain but the showers had not come, leaving us helpless and hopeless.

I needed to get away to a private place…I could not let anyone see my grief. How I received this news would set the tone for everyone in our camp. Though I longed to lie down and weep, I could not. I did not cherish taking apart my dreams here in Hebron.

And, how could more than twelve hundred people be ready in two days?

I turned away, but Abram must have seen the doubt in my eyes, for he softened his voice. "Life will be much easier for all of us. You will see." He came up behind me, put his hands on my neck, and lifted up my hair, which was drenched in sweat. I leaned back into his chest, looking straight ahead. "How long will we stay in Egypt?"

He knew what I was asking. I needed assurance of my future with him. His response was kind, gentle.

"Sarai, God has told me this land is our home, so, we will return to this Land of Promise when the famine passes. We may be gone from two months to two years or more. But, I promise you, we are not forsaking Canaan. We will return."

Those were the words I needed to hear. Every time before I had responded with four simple words: "I will be ready." But today was different. There was not the hope and excitement for my future that I had known those other times. I rested my head in my hands, sat down, and in spite of myself, surrendered to silent sobs.

Our people had broken their backs struggling to resurrect crops from the hard, dry ground. Without the rains, life had become unbearable. No fruit, no vegetables, and no grain supply left. Even our animals looked gaunt. Spirits sank ever lower. The severe famine had stripped the faces around me of health and, even worse, of joy.

I laid down to sleep that last night in Canaan. Thoughts coursed through my mind recalling the many moves I'd made since I married Abram. Packing, unpacking, setting up, and now I would leave the place that meant the most to me. For when Abram and I settled here, as God had directed him, we had finally called somewhere, "Home."

Hebron.

So many memories here.

Eliezer directed the breaking down and packing up. He was a loyal servant of Abram for many years and was a master at making these moves appear less traumatic than they really were. I watched as the goat and camel hair tents were folded and packed among all my household treasures. To see the entirety of my life loaded and tied on carts and camels gave me pause. Though we would travel as a privileged band, safe, and comfortable because of Abram's blessing, we experienced the same need as every village in the area. My husband was perhaps the wealthiest man here, with great riches surpassing most kings in the Canaan region.

Yet today, for all the sadness in my heart at leaving my home, I exhaled and affirmed in my soul that I would look forward to the new camp in a new place and the memories it would surely provide.

And so we departed Hebron, looking forward to the verdant valley of the Nile.

Egypt.

I heard stories of Egypt. Caravan traders had spun tale after tale of a nation advanced through architecture, science, skilled artisans, and medicine. Egypt, they said, "A land of beauty and plenty." A land always blessed and sustained by the mighty Nile.

One trader spoke of brilliant men who, over the ages, built wonders, such as monuments to gods, pyramids, towers, and grand palaces. They worshipped gods created by men while Abram bowed only to the unseen God of Abram. "Egypt," the man continued, "Is ruled by Pharaoh and has become the very pinnacle of civilization."

Another trader regaled me with stories of busy market streets overflowing with stylish apparel, sandals, scarves, and jewelry. The thought of visiting the world market in Egypt brought out the adventurous little girl in me.

All these wonders, so different from my nomadic life…I could not wait for them to tantalize my senses and expand the small world in which I lived. It would be a feast for my eyes, food for my soul. It might even help fill the void that no one sees….

For I was barren.

As we approached the border of Egypt, Abram turned to me. "Sarai, when we enter the city of Memphis, where Pharaoh lives, please say you are my sister."

"Why, Master?"

"Because of your great beauty, if some high ranking official desires you and wants to take you, I would be killed so he could have you."

Because I am so beautiful…Such words should bring me joy, and yet that beauty makes Abram, the chosen of El Shadai, fear for his life? And, does he no longer believe the great promise of God to make a great nation from him and his seed?

"Sarai?"

Do I have the faith to do what he is asking? True, chance and family purity laws gave us the same father but different mothers, so we are half-brother and sister…still….

"Sarai?" Abram said louder than before.

I turned to look into those big adoring eyes, eyes that have always been only on me. "Master, I will surely do as you have asked."

It was settled. Had he mentioned this back in Hebron, I would have had time to ponder the implications of his request. But now…this catches me by surprise.

I didn't remember Abram saying God told him to move, as He had every time before. From Ur of Mesopotamia to Haran, from Haran down to Canaan, we went because God spoke to Abram. This time, the famine brought a fear I had not seen in him before. He trusted God for everything but now, with our food store exhausted….

Had that forced him to think of Egypt as our only survival, even though the Lord God did not say...?

Could it be? Was this move not of God? Was Abram's fear of the

Egyptians stronger than his faith in God's provision? And now this request....

Had Abram planned this charade from the beginning, withholding the details until now because he knew I could not refuse, for we had come too far?

Enough. I must not doubt Abram. I agreed to honor his request. Indeed, what we would say was true. In part, it left out the glaring fact that I was his wife, but I would do as he asked. And I would think on it no more.

Not even to wonder what might happen to me....

I looked ahead to the date palm trees enchanting me, swaying in the breeze. They graced the banks of the Nile, along with flowering mulberry trees, sycamores, papyrus, and water lilies. The fragrance of lotus blooms floated in the air making its way to my senses. So...

This was Egypt.

And the Nile. It flooded every year, making the land rich and fertile. The farmer's blessing and delight. Here among monuments, temples, great pyramids, and reclining Sphinx—my life was new. Everywhere I looked, sights astounded me.

In the distance, towers surrounded by a massive wall reached to the sky. This must be the Great Palace of Pharaoh.

I held captive these images in my mind. I might need them if we ever left Egypt.

Peasants lived in mud huts and brick houses along the great river. They made their homes by gathering mud from the riverbanks, a provision free for the taking. Perhaps Abram and I would not live in our tent complex for long and would purchase a home I could decorate with new furniture, rugs, and ornaments. Hope welled within me. I was happy to be in the city I had only heard about. Now I would experience it firsthand. From Hebron through Beersheba and across the Sinai Desert, we journeyed through the Nile Delta and now into the land of abundance. A stark contrast between the two.

And in the distance was the Jewel of the Nile, Memphis.

Outside the city entrance, Abram found a place suitable to set up camp for the night. The next morning, Abram and I, along with Eliezer, and fifty men dressed in their black desert warrior uniforms, left to go into the city. The men approached the Egyptian officials on camels in two columns of twenty-five men each.

We came to the portal. The guards commanded us to halt.

Eliezer dismounted. "May I speak with your magistrate?"

"Remain here and we shall bring him to you."

Our camels knelt. Abram, the Syrian nomadic sheik, chief of a tribe rich in flocks and herds, dismounted and came to help me stand.

Our guards remained stoic on their camels, looking every part an organized military contingent, dressed in turbans, tunics, trousers, and boots. They exuded an air of confidence and purpose. They were indeed their master's guardians and champions.

The magistrate soon returned along with several high-ranking officials.

Eliezer introduced Abram who gave a slight bow.

"I am Abram, and this is my sister, Sarai. I and all my peoples, trained men, servants, shepherds, slaves, and all their families, came from Canaan, where there is a severe famine. We seek refuge with you until the deprivation in our homeland passes. I would like to ascertain, first if this is possible and second, the amount your royal treasury would require for this consideration."

"Our soldiers made us aware of your arrival yesterday. We know the vastness of your peoples and livestock camped outside. We observed from our lookout post and determined that you were the master and prince of all we beheld. And, we also noted the exquisite beauty of your sister as well."

Abram bowed again.

The magistrate held up his hand. "We will talk to Pharaoh about all you desire. Meet us here tomorrow. In the meantime, you, your sister, and a few of your personal guards, may tour the city. We will assign two soldiers to act as your guide.

Abram inclined his head. "As you wish."

The bustling city of Memphis was alive with activity—people buying and selling their wares, children running back and forth, men leaning against carts telling stories, and women holding their babies. Our entourage caused quite a stir as people turned to stare. Music filled the air giving a festive aura and a welcome gesture.

The smell of meats cooking on open fires called and bakeries emitting tempting aromas stirred within me hunger pangs. I was anxious to sample these delicacies. The frenzied, festival atmosphere gave me a rush, causing me to forget about Hebron and the famine.

Our guides led us through a colonnade that housed shops, so many of them, where one could buy or sell anything…just as the traders had said. I was sure we had only toured a small portion of the market but I signaled Abram that this was quiet enough for one day.

Tired, but armed with fresh provisions, we returned to our staging area. We would have our answer to Abram's request for residency tomorrow.

I could scarcely sleep because of the noise and excitement around us. Did Memphis ever sleep? My mind reveled in the events brought by this day until the lapping waters of the Nile lulled me to deep and restful sleep.

I awakened to hear men talking to Abram outside our tent. I lifted the flap to hear.

"Pharaoh has heard your request. His Majesty desires you and your sister's presence today at the palace."

So we would *not* return to the city gate for Abram's answer but would receive it directly from the palace of Pharaoh.

Abram straightened…so tall and regal. "At what hour shall we attend?"

"You will take your evening meal at the palace and then meet with His Highness. We will be back to escort you at sunset."

"We will be ready."

I closed the flap.

Abram came in to tell me the visitors were palace officials. "Sarai, Pharaoh wishes to meet us today!"

Abram didn't know this news was already a memory in the making for me. I would tell my children someday as I recounted all that happened to us in our travels.

I changed into my finest gown of purple linen trimmed with gold thread, and draped a fuchsia scarf about me. I reached for my pouch of jewelry. So many lovely things Abram had given me through the years. I chose for today gold bracelets, rings with precious stones, and my favorite silver necklace. I dabbed a few drops of oil of persimmon at my ears, breathing in the lovely scent and remembering when Abram brought it to me from En Gedi, by the shores of the Dead Sea.

I released the pins from my hair and ran my fingers through it to let it fall softly at my shoulders. Abram loved it this way. I pinched my cheeks to add color, lined my eyes with charcoal, bathed my lashes with olive oil, and added a touch of charred rose petals mixed with oil to my lips. I slipped into my jeweled sandals.

There, that should be quite enough. I was ready.

Abram stood, waiting for me. He smiled his approval. Dressed in his gold tunic with the black sash and small black cap completed his imperial and princely look.

The palace officials returned as promised to escort us outside the city center. The sounds and scents of the market were behind us as we approached the perimeter of the palace grounds. Massive walls of carved stone stood high, a defensive fortress shielding the royal palace compound high above the city. I turned to view the entire metropolis from there. It was easy to see our own encampment.

As if prearranged, the enormous gates opened. Inside, towers decorated with cornices stood amid buildings and storehouses. Blooming gardens, fountains, and small pools pointed the way to the magnificent residence. There were stables, lodgings, and a private temple with a gold dome. Many smaller palaces stood within the sanctuary, making it a city within itself. Gigantic columns stood like stone sentries guarding the palace. Covered walkways led to each building.

Handsomely dressed royal guards opened the massive doors, which were embellished with enormous iron handles shaped like serpents. The guards moved with precise and deliberate motions. We should not move without further instructions. Pharaoh's ambassador and his entourage stepped forward, laying fresh lily collars about our necks and motioning us to follow them down the long, columned walkway. We turned and entered a room where a lavish display of food waited. Music floated in the air. Harps, lutes, and tambourines provided beautiful sounds. Dancers moved in rhythm. No one looked to notice our entrance. All were intent and lost in their performance.

Abram and I continued to stand, our eyes recording and taking in the spectacle before us. Benches perfectly stationed around the room awaited us. Magnificent art adorned the walls. No one had yet spoken but a servant leaned forward to taste each item on the table, using a different spoon for each: roasted oxen with scallions, legumes, turnips, celery, cucumber, melons, and date cakes. He straightened and signaled the officials, who dismissed him and gave us a lovely gold rimmed plate for our food.

The entertainers exited on cue. The palace officials hosted us and said the pharaoh dined in private, and would call for us later. We ate in silence, speaking only to praise their delicacies. I ignored the stirring in my stomach as I anticipated our meeting with Pharaoh.

We finished our meal. Another signal and officials entered to give us instructions regarding proper protocol for meeting Pharaoh. One gave verbal commands as the other illustrated the instruction. We dared not make a mistake.

"Bow forward, kneel, and make a motion of kissing the ground. But, most important, do not rise until instructed."

I repeated these words several times and prayed I would remember.

A messenger whispered to the head official who stood. "Pharaoh will receive you now."

We followed our attendants toward the grand throne room, lined with Argun palm trees standing tall in their giant white marble vases. Yellow and red flowering plants grew at the base of each. We walked through scrolled double doors and stopped at the foot of the stone steps ascending to the magnificent carved marble and ivory throne.

There, on scarlet cushions, sat Pharaoh.

Pedestals on either side held busts of the Sphinx. Pharaoh's royal headdress was braided gold adorned with an array of exquisite gems. It covered the front of his head and came down to his shoulders. His coarse, long hair was the color of onyx, which matched his intense eyes. In his hand was a golden scepter crowned by the image of a serpent's head. His royal purple robe bore gold emblems and tassels that cascaded onto the stairs.

What a sight for my eyes, taking in every facet of the scene unfolding before me. I would never forget the wonder of it.

And, not just because of the splendor…but because Pharaoh was gazing at me—intently.

His eyes searched me.

I froze for too long. Abram nudged me. Together we bowed, and then knelt as if to kiss the ground, careful not to speak or rise until he invited us.

Which he did, almost immediately. "Please."

We rose.

He motioned us to a candlelit table with reclining couches and rose to join us. A servant assisted and poured wine in the heavy silver goblets. He tasted, nodded, and turned to leave the room, careful to bow and back out so as not to turn his back on his ruler.

Pharaoh studied us. First Abram and then his eyes rested on me once again. Speak O Pharaoh….

"Welcome to my country. I hear you have come from the land of Canaan and desire permission to enter and dwell in my kingdom?"

Abram looked up. "Yes, Majesty."

"I pray your journey went well?"

"Indeed, well."

"And have you a wife Abram?"

My heart raced as I looked to my husband.

"I have traveled here with my sister, Sarai, and my nephew."

That was close.

"And this is the sister you mentioned?"

Abram looked down and took a sip from the goblet in his hand.

"Yes Lord, my sister, Sarai." He picked up the linen napkin and wiped his mouth.

The eyes of both men fell at once on me. My face reddened.

Pharaoh smiled. "When my officials came yesterday telling of your arrival with dominions of people and livestock, they were most struck, not by the number of your peoples, but by the splendid beauty of your sister. Each one spoke in turn saying, 'She is, without a doubt, the most striking woman we have ever seen in your kingdom.'"

I leaned forward to hear more as Abram brought his goblet to his lips again.

"Seeing their reaction to such beauty, I ordered that I must see you. And this is why you were invited here. And now, seeing the truth for myself, I am in total agreement with their assessment."

His words rested in midair as he studied me again. "Abram, I cannot allow another to take her as a wife."

Thank you, Pharaoh!

"So"—he paused, as though carefully choosing his words—"With your blessing, I will bring her into my palace harem to become my wife."

I straightened on the couch. Had my ears misheard? I looked to Abram—he was powerless, trapped in a state of shock and utter confusion. He could not speak out nor could he refuse Pharaoh. In this moment, I saw my strong husband as I'd never seen him before…

Helpless.

He knew, as did I, that this act would bring danger to me. And yet we both knew he could not refuse or suggest an alternative. In all our years together, this was the first time he could not protect me. Caught in his own web of deceit, he sat, cloaked in silence, wearing his panic like a robe.

Ignoring Abram's silence, Pharaoh continued. "Abram, as Sarai's brother, you may live in my kingdom as long as you wish, under my care, protection, and provision. I would not think of charging you fees! But I, on the other hand, will pay you a handsome bridal price."

It was then I expected Abram to speak up with the truth. He would lose me and I would forever be a possession of the ruler of Egypt, never to sleep in his tent again.

"Even though I am aware that you have much wealth, this dowry will make you an even stronger prince for it will include lavish amounts of gold and silver, male and female servants, livestock including sheep, cattle, male and female donkeys, and oxen."

"Lord Highness." Abram's voice was softer now, and I understood he had surrendered me.

"This is a small price to pay for the most beautiful woman my eyes have beheld."

"Yes, Lord Pharaoh." Abram swallowed hard. His face reddened.

"Permit Sarai to remain here, even tonight."

"Yes, Majesty." His eyes darted to mine and then away too soon.

Abram's deception had spared his life and garnered him even more wealth. But what about me? What about the sanctity of our marriage?

I closed my eyes to block out what I had witnessed.

And thus, it was so.

I became betrothed to Pharaoh in the Great Palace of Egypt. Invited as a dinner guest but retained as a resident bride…because of my husband's deception.

He turned and went to his new home in Egypt.

Without me.

A servant girl appeared and bowed.

"This way, My Lady."

There was nothing to do but follow. "Thank you."

"I am Nafrini, your attendant."

She took me down the hallway leading me to my uncertain future. Passed apartment doors and common areas we went. She paused to unlock the door in front of her, which opened to a lavish apartment. Oh my. Sumptuous furnishings and details dazed me. Such a long journey from my tent in the desert. I could not speak. I turned to Nafrini.

She smiled. "Sleep well Sarai. Tomorrow I come for you to begin preparations."

"Thank you."

What preparations?

Reality gnawed at me. Without the protective covering of my husband,

and with our half-truth working its course, I was at the whims and mercy of a ruler I did not know, ruling a nation I knew less.

I sat on the bed for I knew not how long, numb to two things—my situation, and the bountiful loveliness enfolding me in this room. My eyes dampened with questioning tears. How could my life with Abram end like this?

Would I be here forever, never to embrace my beloved again? I missed him, but would he miss me. Was his love bigger than my fear? Without evidence of his love, my fear might overcome me, making me helpless and unable to survive. The very epicenter of my world was at risk. I knew not the time or place the pharaoh would take me but ever certain he would.

I knew only that I was abandoned.

Early the next morning, Nafrini awakened me with a warm wet cloth to my face and a tray of breakfast items. "Sarai, your time of bride purification will start immediately and continue for many sunsets. Pharaoh has arranged for Nile traders to bring materials for your new palace wardrobe: jewels, footwear, fabrics, and anything you desire for your pleasure and beauty. And, there are things here in this chest that you may choose."

I pulled the tray close. Nafrini held up her hand passionately to stop me. "Wait! Please!" She pulled a spoon from her pocket, tasted my food, and waited a few moments before pushing the tray back in front of me. She nodded approval, smiled, and left.

I looked at the food before me. What had Abram eaten for breakfast and who brought it? Could all the treasures arriving from the palace make up for his empty bed last night? Or for the sacrifice of his wife? Yes, he'd said if suitors approached for my hand in marriage, he would propose a very long engagement where I would remain in his house. He planned to store enough supplies and be gone from Egypt before the date of a proposed marriage. But, he never dreamed Pharaoh would take me into his harem. Or...

Had he?

Soon Nafrini came again.

"First we go to the bathhouses, and then attendants will groom your hair and adorn you with ornaments suited for a princess."

I walked with her toward the bathhouse. Here girls and women of incredible beauty soaked and swam in pools filled with fragrant blooms. Lotus perfume hung in the air. Its delicate scent quieted my uneasy spirit for the moment.

Afterwards, maidens colored my hair with henna giving it a radiant sheen. They brushed and braided it with jewels and pinned it high on my head. I had never worn a headdress like this, carefully woven into my hair like a halo. A wide collar laden with pearls, emeralds, diamonds, and rubies adorned my neck. I looked like a princess on the outside, but inside I was a frightened little girl.

The grand tour of the palace grounds was next. It took the better part of three days. My legs tired from all the walking. The interior of the great palace was opulent—boasting fine, colorful linens on overdressed beds with beautiful canopied wood. Carpets covered most of the tiled floor, brilliant mosaics adorned the walls and niches, and there was an abundance of Egyptian art revealing the history of the country.

The library was filled with books, scrolls, and parchments, too many to number. The museum featured busts and oil paintings of former Pharaohs and the walls bore maps of Egypt. The stairs and hallways were embellished with gold finials and scrollwork. Every detail was finished to perfection. Who had designed and decorated this imposing edifice? It must have taken centuries.

Outside were a vast number of stables, acres of livestock, storehouses overflowing with grain and plenty, and lodgings for the estate workers. I saw Pharaoh's great chariots of gold, awaiting his call. Such a powerful figure, this ruler of Egypt. And I, Sarai from Canaan, was here on the inside, looking out beyond the palace gates that kept my beloved from me. All I had dreamed on the journey to Egypt I now experienced, but my heart longed to be with my husband, in a goat-hair desert tent.

I began the first round of protocol with other women recently taken into the pharaoh's harem. The bridal preparation entailed a tight daily schedule including a regimen of hibiscus soaks, oil massages, mud baths, salt scrubs, dietary guidelines, and hair and skin treatments. What wondrous news to discover it would be months before I completed this obligation, making me ready for *the* call.

One morning, another girl attended me at breakfast saying Nafrini was ill. Her stomach ailed her. Had some of the food she tasted been tainted?

I heard talk among the servants at the bathhouse that an infection touched many of palace staff and was spreading. Even Pharaoh, they said, was afflicted in some way.

I was grateful to remain healthy. Our daily schedule came to a halt as the plague broadened. I checked my skin daily to make sure I was not infected. I offered to help but was forbidden to mingle with the others. New slaves and servants were added to the staff but soon they were stricken. Some days the only food options were fruit and nuts as the cooks could not perform their duties. Doctors and medical scholars came to evaluate the traumatic plague. Panic loomed, and I saw fear in the eyes of all those I encountered. Everyone had been touched in some way by this strange malady.

The ladies of the women's quarters were quarantined to our rooms but our doors were open to hear the doctor's remedies. It was difficult they said, because there was not one major ailment, but rather many kinds of plagues, which confounded them.

Jaundice, leprosy, smallpox, and skin infections were treated from the flowers of the henna tree. Its poultice created an instant scab to close open wounds with its antiseptic properties. It provided a cooling agent for burning skin. Honey was used to treat open wounds, thus preventing the spread of infection to other parts of the body.

Gum from the acacia tree was for stomach, bowel, bladder diseases, and ulcers. Coriander seeds had pain-relieving properties for headaches, muscle pain, and stiffness. This paste helped mouth ulceration and made a poultice for other ulcers. Its essential oil would remove toxins and stimulate circulation.

All these remedies, but nothing worked. No cure came.

The palace was collapsing. The invasion seized its residents, holding them hostage, with no release in sight.

Early one morning, a call came for me to go to the throne room. I hastened to follow the attendant down the long hallway. Panic gripped me. Why was I called? I entered the great room, where the once-powerful Pharaoh sat pale and drawn in his regal chair. His appearance was remarkably different from the last time I stood here. On either side, his council members and court, all somewhat paled, flanked him.

I bowed and knelt to the ground before him. It seemed an unusually long time before I heard him speak.

"Rise."

His voice was changed. Weaker.

"Yes, Majesty."

"Sarai."

He took a deep breath and as he exhaled, I saw sorrow in his eyes.

"A great sickness has befallen my household. I have called medical scholars and the best doctors of medicine available to me. After weeks and now months of thorough examination, today I have received startling evidence that involves you."

"No, Lord, no!"

"Indeed, yes. This great plague of many diseases has affected everyone in some way. Everyone…except you."

"Oh no, Majesty,"

"We all suffer greatly."

"But surely nothing implicating me!"

"My council said this plague began manifesting itself the day you arrived."

I stared but did not respond. My heartbeat pounded in my ears and the echo of his words accused me.

"Sarai, I must ask you. Is there something you know that causes this epidemic to seize the whole of my kingdom?"

I felt the color drain from my face. My throat was dry. My hands were ice cold. I could not bear to look in his eyes. My knees almost buckled. I swallowed hard and forced a whispered response. "Yes, Lord."

"Then let us hear it!" His voice now rang with contempt.

"My Lord King, truly you were deceived, for I am Abram's half-sister but...I am also his wife."

An icy atmosphere griped the room. I looked down—convicted by the truth of my words. The silence was deafening.

I looked up again to see Pharaoh's white knuckles gripping the arms of his throne. His words reverberated out of the room and filled the hallways. He shouted orders for his emissaries to bring Abram at once. His voice had not failed him now.

His stern look ordered me to remain in place. I stood as a statue until Abram arrived. As my husband entered the throne room, he glanced at me as if to say, *"Forgive me Sarai."* His abrupt abandonment of me to save himself still hurt…but I was happy to see him. Now I feared even more for we would both pay the price for Abram's deceit. We might be imprisoned, tortured—, or worse.

Why had Abram insisted?

He looked ahead and bowed low to the ground before the pharaoh of Egypt.

"Abram, what is this you have brought upon my house?"

Abram rose. "What, Lord?"

"Why did not you tell me Sarai was your wife? And indeed why did you say, 'She is my sister?'"

My legs still trembled. Would he have us both killed?

Pharaoh repeated the tragic events that had overtaken his palace and told of my confession. "You have brought all this to my kingdom, and I, I could have taken her as my wife!"

Abram rose. "My Lord, she is indeed my sister but of a different mother. Because of her great beauty, I feared some high official might desire her and I knew it would cost my life. That is why I said she is my sister. Never, did I think that you, O Pharaoh, would choose her for your own."

Pharaoh raged. "But I did, and now this plague ravishes my house!"

Abram's voice grew ever stronger. Now it was his words flanking the walls of the palace. "I fear for the lives of everyone in your entire household for this is truly a judgment of the Lord God, whom I serve. He has brought this disease upon your household. It is His warning that Sarai should not be taken as a wife by any other!"

I caught my breath. Abram's proclamation about God's protection resonated in me. I could see in Pharaoh's face that he was stricken at Abram's words. He was a man undone.

I welcomed the moment of silence. I was comforted to hear Abram speak his bold proclamation without shame or apology. No matter what happened now, the message of God rang loud in Pharaoh's ears, and the truth rested in his hands. Our God was not to be taken lightly. His power had penetrated the high walls of this fortress and brought the most powerful man in Egypt to his knees.

He had no choice but to release us. There was no telling what the Lord God would do if he harmed us now.

Pharaoh had run out of options. He could do but two things: kill us or let us go. Harming us would mean surrendering his entire palace to the disease that threatened both him and his weakened empire.

Pharaoh finally spoke. "Abram, get thee out of my country at once! My agents will escort you out of my city. As for the many treasures I paid for Sarai, you make keep."

He motioned me away with his hand, eager to be freed from any remembrance of me. "Now then, here is your wife. Take her and be gone!"

Abram bowed low. "I pray, Lord, that the health of you and your household will be restored the moment we depart."

We left the palace. I did not look back.

Safely at our camp, we packed in haste, while the armed palace guards watched. Our exodus drew much more attention than our arrival, for we were now more than a small village. Carts and camels loaded high with grain and other provisions lined up like a parade. There were enough goods to sustain our entire company for over a year—another gift from Pharaoh. Even if the famine was not completely over in Hebron, we could survive in the desert plains of Negev.

I was seated high upon a cart with a covering for shade, ready to depart. Eliezer came with two young maidens. He stepped close to tell me that my handmaiden Nissa had died during the time I was in the palace. I had forgotten to ask for her when I returned this morning. She had served me for many years and treated me as her child. I was saddened to hear this news. He stood quietly as the news sank in. I looked again to him. Eliezer had something else to say—"Sarai, I watched the young women behind me and have brought them to you in hopes that one may please you to take Nissa's place."

I questioned both girls but I knew the young Hagar was the one to serve me. I dismissed the other girl and informed Eliezer of my choice. Hagar joined me in my shaded cart as we left her homeland to return to mine.

The servant girl was quiet, making me grateful. I had much to consider regarding my time here. In my solitude, the glory of Egypt was short-lived and behind me as quick as a breath. If only it could have been different, with Abram and me living here, enjoying the beauty and comforts Egypt offered.

But that was not to be.

The monuments and sights of the city grew smaller, and I set my focus on Canaan. I would never forget the impact Egypt had on my life, or how Abram's God watched over and delivered me.

We had begun our migratory tent life years ago, after Abram followed God's call, first to leave Ur in Mesopotamia until another call from God led us to the Land of Promise. Our first camp was at Shechem, where God promised the land to Abram. And he believed this as much as he believed God would provide a son for him through me, even though the entirety of the land was inhabited by Canaanites who did not worship the true and living God. There Abram built an altar. But in time, God told him to move again. And so we went to a place near Bethel and put up our tents. There Abram built an altar. How long would we be there? For that was not the final destination God had called Abram to all those years ago.

We moved southward yet again, following another call of the Lord God. How many moves did I have left in me? I had supervised the packing of the elements of my homestead so many times, watched them carefully placed on beasts of burden, submitting to Abram and his God.

Would the moving never stop? When would I have a place to call my home and rest in the comfort that I would never have to move again? We lived the Bedouin life and traveled so many miles through the hot and dusty desert to a place called Negev. There in Hebron, God told Abram it was to be our dwelling place. It suited me fine. If Abram was happy, I obliged. My husband did what he always did. He built an altar and we remained there and called it our home until the great famine came, drawing us to Egypt.

Hagar spoke only when I spoke to her. Sometimes I forgot she accompanied me. She brought water and tended to my every need. I had chosen well.

Days passed and one day I asked about her family. They were all slaves in Egypt. She had been separated from them as a youth when she became a slave in the Royal Palace of Pharaoh. Other servants in the palace, she said, were the only family she knew. I told her I was barren. She knew I had no children with me so I made this known to her. I saw sadness in her dark chestnut eyes with my announcement. I changed the subject.

With our journey almost completed, we would settle at home in Hebron once again. This was the first time I could say I was coming home and know where it was. I had made a life there and everything would not be strange and foreign as it was in Egypt. I would not be an alien. Perhaps this would be our final resting place and we would finish our life here. If Abram were content, then I would prepare myself to walk in step with his desire and his God would be my only God. I would serve no other.

Abram's walk and his faith would show me the way.

Hagar proved attentive to my every need and I was grateful. I became dependent on her, for she made my daily life easier. Like Nafrini in Egypt, Hagar anticipated my need before I asked. We would get along well and in this, I rejoiced.

Everything seemed as it had before we left Hebron. Each night Abram went to his altar to call upon the name of the Lord. I had not seen his ritual for many months and it did my heart good. Had this been his nightly routine in the pagan land of Egypt? How I missed seeing him go to his altar in the morning and in the coolness of the evening. Perhaps he had prayed in his bed at night, or made an altar in his tent.

No matter, I was sure he had made an altar in his heart.

One day, soon after leaving our tent, Abram came in, grinning and out of breath.

"God renewed the promise of a son to inherit all this wealth and carry on the generations from here to eternity!"

"That's good, Abram. I am glad Yahweh God still speaks to you." There it was again. Abram's seed. His legacy, yes, but the curse of my womb would not produce the promised heir.

This womb would bring Abram no sons. My significance, my worth, was nothing. Other women honored their husbands with many sons—heirs. I longed for the day I would do the same. Now…

Why had I been barren! It was a shame I would never escape. But Abram never looked at me with anything but love.

As he looked at me now.

"Sarai, God told me, 'Look to the North, South, East, and West—to all the land you can see. I will give it to all to your descendants forever. In addition, I will make your descendants as prolific as the dust of the earth.'"

The North, South, East, and West. That included all of Canaan, from Dan in the north to Beersheba in the south, from the river Egypt to the great river Euphrates. The Kenites, Kenizzites, Rephaites, Amorites, Canaanites, Girgashites, and Jebusites occupied these lands! And yet God told my husband He would give his descendants this new land.

More pressure on me.

But Abram believed. And so I hoped and waited, in Canaan, the place where God showed Abram this promise. Days, weeks, and months went by. Soon years had passed, and still there was no child of promise born. Years turned into a decade, and my hope for the child who held the key to blessings for all people of the earth was all but lost. My childbearing years passed, and I grew old.

God had forgotten me.

While I lived trapped in the circumstances of my curse, Abram's faith grew stronger. I learned much from watching him, but even his presence couldn't change the fact that I was alone and lost in the middle of the promise. I was ensnared in the heart of God's plan and my unsteady faith.

I busied myself with weaving, cooking, baking, and helping the servants prepare food needed for each meal. Always with Hagar by my side. Abram communed with God. He said they had a covenant. And I?

I had my doubts.

The promise could not be fulfilled...because of me. Abram couldn't have a descendant without me. He was faithful to me and never wanted to take another wife, even though he was free to do so but his love for me and his faith in God's promises restrained him.

I watched Abram age and my heart began to ache for him even more than it did for me. What of his hope? His need? I cried out to Abram's God. "Give Abram a son!" But Abram had not lost heart. My husband still went to the altar every day as if today were going to be the day.

I *had* to do something.

One day, I heard him and looked outside to hear his cry.

"O LORD God, hear my plea. I have waited for Your promise so long. Won't You please, please send me a son before I am too old to teach him Your way? Oh how I need a son—I need a son, a son...."

It broke my heart to see him lying face down with his chest heaving across his altar. My heart pounded and an uprising welled in me as I clinched my fist. "I *will* help God and His beloved Abram!"

The promise said a seed would come from Abram's body. Perhaps I was not to be the mother, after all. What would be the greatest sacrifice I could give my Abram?

A surrogate.

This had been practiced since the beginning of time…a child born of someone else's womb but belonging to another.

So there, in the cool of the day, my heart made a vow—I would do anything, anything, to give Abram his son. Why had it taken me so long to figure this out? The solution had been right before my eyes! It was so obvious now. How long did I hold up God's plans to bless my husband? Hadn't I known I was childless? Now, I could provide the child of promise!

Hagar, my Egyptian handmaiden, walked by and instantly, I knew.

Abram returned from his time at the altar. His face was wet. He had been weeping. I saw weariness in his face and for the first time, I did not see hope.

I asked him to sit down by me. "The Lord has prevented me from having children but that should not prevent you. I am providing a way for you to father your Child of Promise. Go and sleep with my servant, Hagar. Perhaps I can have children through her. My love for you will not wane but God's promise to you will be fulfilled in this way."

Abram was silent as he processed what I had offered. He knew it was a sacrifice of love from me to him. Would he accept or would his faith in God prevent him? At last, he stood and nodded, thus approving my proposal. He did not say I must ask God, or I must not do this thing.

He waited in silence.

I went to Hagar. "My husband is very old and he needs a son. I am unable to bear children, and I want you to lie with him for a child."

She looked at me as if I had lost my mind. Her eyes were wide and she did not blink. She bowed her head and stared at her feet. "As My Mistress desires, so will I do. My mission is to serve and I will do as you ask." She turned and went to her tent.

And I sent Abram to her.

In all our years together, no one had come between us. Abram never had eyes for another but now, and for this purpose, and in this moment, it seemed right. It was a bittersweet act. I gave Hagar to Abram as a second wife.

When she conceived—and it happened quickly, she came to tell me.

"I am with Abram's child!"

I saw pride on her face. My sweet and gentle servant girl had changed. For the first time in her life, she had something I didn't...and probably never would. Every day she relished her position. She neglected her duties and acted as if she were the mistress of my home.

One day I made a simple request and she spit words at me.

"I despise you!"

She lived no longer to serve me, but rather the child that grew within her. But I held my tongue. For I knew the truth. According to the law, that child she carried did not belong to her.

That child belonged to me!

Her taunting continued as she rolled her eyes at my requests and delayed in responding to my wishes. She walked away before I finished talking. I caught her watching Abram and making unnecessary trips outside while he worked. Jealousy and loathing became my constant companions, all but driving me to madness.

Soon, my anger focused on Abram. How could he have taken Hagar? And how could he treat her with such honor? Did he not see what she had become? How she treated me?

One day I walked outside to see them in the distance—he placed one hand on her stomach and one up to the Heavens, as if praying a blessing on the unborn child. When he came in, I could not control my anger. "You should have declined my offer and said no! Did you ever think how much this would hurt me? Have you given any consideration to what this is doing to me?"

"Sarai, it was your idea, was it not?"

"But I did not know how this would change *her*! She no longer respects me. She insults me and at the very sight of her, I am angry. I don't think I even want this child for I have no part in it. Please, just send her away."

"She is your servant and you should do with her as you please." He walked away.

I wanted Abram to put his arms around me and say, "Oh, dear Sarai, I am so sorry. You are my beloved. I will talk to Hagar and make sure this never happens again. It is not right for her to treat you this way. I will not allow her to disgrace you in your own home." But he did not move toward me or speak those words.

He disowned and gave it back to me. I wanted his protection and to know that I was still his treasured, number-one wife. What I gained was more disappointment.

Fine, so be it.

I put extra work on Hagar and made her life so miserable that she ran away. And when she did, I was glad! My plan had not worked. My once happy home had turned into a battlefield, where my servant and I both vied for the position of being Abram's favored wife.

Now all I wanted was to be rid of this upstart and her child.

My peace did not last long. It was only days before another servant came to tell me Hagar had returned. I was not prepared for another interruption in my private world with Abram. I told the servant to tell her to wait outside until I decided how I would handle this. This was my chance to deny her and the child she carried back into the safety of my peaceful home. I thought of the miserable days I endured her hateful behavior, and yet…

I knew Abram would prefer to have her nearby, at least until the birth of his heir.

What were my options? I could deny this insolent slave, but that would hurt my husband. I could allow her, but that would hurt me.

Even as I struggled, though, a harsh truth struck me.

I had options.

Hagar had none.

If I rose above my frustrations and set proper rules for her before permitting her back, it might work. I asked Abram's God to let this be the right decision.

And without further thought, I sent for Hagar.

I almost did not recognize the woman who stood in my presence. Gone was the arrogant slave girl of a few days before. This young woman could not bring herself to look at me. I sat waiting until she found her voice, gaining strength to speak. At last, she raised her eyes to meet mine.

Her very presence before me spoke humility. Her voice cracked. "Please My Lady, can you…can you… forgive me?"

I nodded.

"I will honor you with all my being and walk with meekness before you. I will not interfere with your and Abram's life. I am grateful to be received again, after the way I treated you."

I paused, taking in all she said. She must have practiced her responses all the way from the wilderness that led her back. I could not know if she was repentant but her words touched a chord within me. I would have to give her another chance. Things would be very different now.

"Is it well with you, Hagar?"

"It is well."

"Then go to your tent to refresh yourself and sleep in peace. We shall talk more tomorrow."

Hagar was respectful and worked harder than she ever did before—but the die was cast. I watched but found no reason to fault her. As I saw her belly grow, her time to deliver grew near, and again, I could think of only one thing: Why, oh why had I given her to Abram? It was true that she didn't have a choice. Still….

It pained me every time I saw Abram looking at the mother of his child of promise. And deep inside, I wailed.

O God, what have I done?

Hagar's time of delivery came, and midwives attended in her tent. I looked out to see Abram pacing. He was eighty-six years old, yet looked like a young man awaiting the birth of his first child. I heard the cry of a newborn and the midwives came out to say, "Abram, Hagar has given you a son!"

Abram put his hands to his face and dropped to his knees. He bent his head to the ground and wept. Soon he rose to hold his son. I heard him tell the infant of the long wait for his arrival. He put his hand on the babe's head and blessed him. They named him Ishmael—God hears.

In the following days, Abram was careful not to parade his pleasure in front of me, yet I saw how he found time to visit Hagar's tent to nestle, play, and talk with the child.

Hagar, of course, was overjoyed.

And I? I was left out of the joyous celebration. In their happy family, there was no place for me. Hagar nursed and cuddled her baby, while Abram watched, eyes shining. And soon I came to understand.

The child would not be mine after all.

I was used to having all of Abram's attention and affection. Now there was another wife and their baby to share and fill his life. For the first time, there was a part of his life that did not include me.

Before long, jealousy overtook me. Abram and I argued every time we spoke. The love I always saw in his eyes was changing, and I could not stop it…or my angry words. All I could think was…*this is my reward for helping God?* Just see if I would do that again, ever!

And so I remained on the outside, invisible and alone. We were a house divided but…Abram had his son.

Thirteen years passed, and as I lost my happy life alone with Abram, Ishmael was growing into a young man. He was tall and lean, like his father. They spent time together as Abram taught him to be a hunter in the nearby forest.

I spent my days on the outside of the promise, looking inward because of what I created yet could not participate. The consequence of running ahead of God was a daily reminder. With no hope for a change, I settled into the life I had created.

Then God came to Abram and made another covenant! This one He sealed as never before.

Abram came in from his altar visit. "The Lord God has changed my name! I will now be called Abraham, which means 'Father of Many Nations.'" He was breathless.

I had heard visitors outside the tent addressing him.

"God has changed your name too! You will now be Sarah, 'Mother of Nations! And you will bear a son.'"

I stared at my husband. Me, a mother? Not just of one child, but of many nations? How could that be? How could that ever be? Surely, Abram…no, Abraham heard wrong.

God told him I would have a child from my own body and kings would come from me. I was eighty-nine and he was ninety-nine years old! This was impossible for me to accept as possible.

I looked in Abraham's warm and gentle eyes and saw…he believed.

God said He had already blessed Ishmael, who would be the father of a great nation but that our son, Abraham's and mine would also be the father of a great nation. And God said we should name our son Isaac—laughter.

I couldn't help myself. I laughed. How could such a thing be possible? God's promise wasn't for me! After all, He had never spoken to me, but rather to Abraham. Now to hear such a proclamation, knowing my youth had passed and it was impossible for me to conceive, I laughed within, but Someone heard. The Lord God had read my thoughts. Abraham laughed too, but not with unbelief.

I was exposed. Caught in my unbelief, I was afraid. When He asked Abraham why I laughed, I denied it. But I will never forget God's response.

"Yes, you did laugh! Is there anything too hard for God?"

Far from causing fear, these words sent overflowing joy. This time I did not laugh. I wept, for I believed! By this same time next year, I would have my son!

And then it happened. One day….

I felt a child move in my womb!

The stirring within for the past weeks had not been an illness after all. I counted the days that passed and realized this was the promise fulfilled. The time of delivery would be the same time of the year as I overheard the promise. This was the most marvelous moment of my life. For Abraham, it would be his second time of wonderment but for me, every aspect of giving birth was a gift straight from heaven. After forty years of promises, God had visited me.

I treasured each day of my pregnancy, and when I bore Abraham his true Son of Promise, my joy was complete.

Yes, complete…except for one small thing.

The constant conflict with Hagar and Ishmael.

For now, there were two sons and two wives in the house of Abraham, all still begging his attention.

About the time of Isaac's weaning, Abraham planned a great festival to celebrate. I saw Ishmael mocking little Isaac and became enraged. I thought about him, the first-born, receiving the lion's share of Abraham's estate. It was more than I could bear. To see Ishmael taking all that should be reserved for my Isaac could not be the will of God, could it? I vowed it could not. Why had Abraham not realized this? Must I always be the one to put an end to this madness?

My life was filled with what ifs. What if I had waited on the Lord? What if I had been more proactive in my faith and made my own altars, would The God of Abraham have spoken directly to me too? What if I had not let Hagar sleep with my—yes, my—Abraham? Then I wouldn't worry about him thinking of someone else. What if Isaac were Abraham's only son? What if—I couldn't bear to face it anymore.

And that's when I knew. I couldn't. I had made the mistake of my life to complete Abraham's dream…but in doing so, I had given up mine. Now, I wanted Hagar removed from my sight so my what ifs would not be so painful.

If I could put her out of my house, out of my sight, erase the past, and forget her altogether, life would be perfect.

I confronted Abraham. "This seed of yours from Hagar, I cannot stand him in my presence any longer. Please send them away from my sight."

My husband did not answer me, but turned away. My eyes followed him as he shuffled to the altar to inquire of God. I knew why.

He loved Ishmael.

Early the next morning, I saw Abraham with Hagar and Ishmael, holding a lamp in the early darkness. They stood in a little circle. Abraham's arms ensconced them. He was praying and blessing them. He gave them a kiss and sent them away with but a small portion of food and water. I saw his hand waving until they disappeared in the distance.

He was quiet. He grieved for many days that turned into years. I could not decide if my latest plan was a blessing or a curse. True, I had Abraham all to myself with little Isaac, but we didn't have all of him. For part of his heart departed with Hagar and Ishmael. Of this, I was sure, and it was then—I realized the terrible truth.

My what ifs would always be with me.

I am now an old woman. My years are one-hundred-and twenty-seven, and my time is nigh. As I look back, I have known many blessings.

My Isaac was more than I ever could imagine for a son.

But I have known regret, too.

And fear.

My foolishness and lack of waiting on the Lord God created conflict between me and Hagar—and between our sons. And I grow ever more certain that this conflict will *never* end.

I am ready to meet my Maker. I look forward to the paradise where I will be new in God's heaven. My struggle on this earth is over and I go in peace.

At my last breath, I do what I should have done all those years ago….

I surrender my will to God, asking only one thing: that He continues His work in the nations that come from these two Sons of Promise.

Read Sarah's Story in Genesis 11-23, Hebrews 11:8-13

Chapter 3

Hagar

THOUGH I WALKED amid a throng of people, I was alone....

Such was the life of a slave. I had not the companionship of my family. I knew not where they were. I came into this life with no personal freedom, born at the lowest level of society here in the great metropolis of Memphis. Egypt's capital was the largest settlement in the world. Or so said the Nile traders.

It was hot and it was crowded as I walked among sheep, cattle, donkeys, and camels. I swatted the flies and ignored the stench hovering in the air. Today I would step into a great unknown, to leave my past behind me. As was the plight of all slaves, I followed a master. My new master.

A man named Abram.

I watched as oxen-pulled carts loaded with possessions, provisions, and all the wealth that accompanied a royal family were staged to leave the city they had inhabited for mere months. There were so many soldiers, slaves, servants, and children moving about. I broke through the chaos of those who waited...as did I, to begin a new life away from the land of our birth—to see Prince Abram and his wife, Sarai. He helped her to the covered cart at the head of this great multitude. I moved closer for another look.

Beautiful.

No...Spectacular.

Oh, I how I envied her personal attendants, for to serve a woman such as she would be a dream.

But though a slave, I carried hope and the dream of a better life, someday, somewhere. More than that, I believed I had a destiny beyond the life of a slave. This hope almost frightened me, but I tucked it deep in my heart. I had endured many hardships and losses, and yet I did not dread this change. For it might hold the key to unlock my destiny.

I had belonged to and served in the house of Pharaoh. Then, one day a few months ago, he gave me to Prince Abram from Canaan—for the love of Sarai, Abram's sister.

When she took residence there, the Royal Palace was under the spell of her beauty. The next day I discovered I was part of the bride-gift Pharaoh gave to Abram. I, along with livestock, palace treasures, and many other servants and slaves went to him at his campsite along the Nile.

Out of a royal palace and into a tent.

I learned that Abram and Sarai, along with their entourage, had entered Memphis to seek refuge from a famine in the east. When Pharaoh saw Sarai, he was overcome with passion for her. What joy there was when Abram said she was his sister! Pharaoh took Sarai into his harem as an intended wife.

Abram came to Egypt as a welcomed and honored prince, but now…

He was expelled, scorned, and detested by the pharaoh. He would leave with even more wealth than when he arrived, but palace guards surrounded us now with weapons—making sure Abram and his entourage moved out of Egypt.

Now.

Little wonder considering all that had transpired….

In the months since I left the palace, I adjusted to living in tents and following Abram's way of life. Because of my familiarity with the markets and Egyptian language, I was elevated from performing menial chores to accompanying Abram's buyers to the great market in the city center. I showed them preferred shops, where fair prices and value could be had.

The market was alive with workers' tales, gossip, and news of their masters. One day, I heard disturbing news from the palace.

A calamity reigned and the fear was great.

An unknown sickness plagued Pharaoh's household. One by one, the Royal Family and palace workers fell ill. And yet, though the sickness had reached uncontrollable proportion in the palace, no one outside the palace walls had been affected!

When we returned to Abram's encampment, I shared the terrible news with other slaves from the palace. They were distressed…and yet, from what they said, Abram did not seem to know. At least, he showed no sign of concern for his beloved sister if he did.

I fought back the temptation to tell him. It was not my place, but I worried...what would happen to me if Abram discovered I knew and didn't tell? Or worse, if I told him and it proved untrue?

Not two days later, we came back from the market to find Pharaoh's guards standing like statues outside Abram's tent. They were there to escort him to the palace, but they emanated fear and duress. They ordered that he must come to Pharaoh in that very moment.

Could this dilemma be connected to the sickness at the palace? The one that hovered over the Royal Residence like a blanket of death. Had Sarai fallen to the disease?

I feared the worst as Abram left for the palace.

Soon he was back from his audience with Pharaoh. And Sarai was with him!

My eyes froze on her. So *this* was Sarai. The one who gave new meaning to the word beauty, for it was not sufficient to describe her. Radiant and vibrant, she fairly glowed. She was not ill, nor harmed in any way.

Relief swept me knowing she was well. But then the whispers started. The illness had not touched her, but she had been its cause!

Abram had lied to Pharaoh.

Sarai, as he had said, was his half-sister. But what he had not told Pharaoh was that she was also his wife!

The God they served struck Pharaoh and his palace for taking Abram's wife into his harem. Now she was returned to her husband, but we all were to pay a price for their deception.

"Eliezer!" Abram's voice boomed. "Make ready all the servants, slaves, families, and livestock. Break apart our camp and pack all our possessions. For we must exit Egypt this very day!"

I gasped, as did others. How could all the pieces of our lives here be disassembled and loaded in this short time?

Abram's trusted attendant, Eliezer, acted at once, setting in motion everything required for our exodus.

So here we were. Waiting...the city gates ahead—and soon the palace, and all our stories—behind us.

We slaves mumbled. Had the great God of Abram sent this plague to punish Pharaoh or to protect Sarai from becoming his wife? Would this God deliver and keep her safe, even though she and Abram lied concerning her kinship to Abram?

Deep in my heart, I trembled. Would I meet this God above all Gods, as they had proclaimed? Where did He reside that He could track them in every country and space?

I had questions of this God.

"Hagar."

I spun around. Eliezer stood near. He snapped his fingers. "Come with me."

I followed him and another slave girl to where Sarai waited, in the tented cart that protected her from the sun. She sat ensconced on colorful cushions.

Eliezer signaled us to wait, and then approached her. "My Mistress, I regret to tell you that your aged handmaiden, Nissa, has passed in your absence. I bring two maidens, whom I have watched during the last months, and believe you will find one of them a loyal handmaiden."

Sarai sat tall in her cart, head erect, almost touching the curtain top. She gazed upon us, and we lowered our eyes to the ground. When she spoke, her voice was loud and clear but carried a soft melodic air. "Eliezer, I am saddened to hear this news of Nissa, for she served me many years. Yet I am grateful you have made plans concerning my well being and comfort. Let me now speak with these young women."

So this was why he'd brought us here! My heart pounded, for had I not wished for such a chance in the very moments before?

He waved us forward.

We moved to stand before Sarai. Was it a dream? Was this one-step closer to my destiny?

I looked into the face of this extraordinary woman, and knew why Pharaoh had claimed her for his own.

She raised her hand. "Tell me where and with whom you have served, and the training you have received."

I stepped back and waited my turn. I did not want to be first. I needed a moment to think. After the first girl had finished, I moved forward and bowed. When I lifted my head, I noticed Sarai's pleasing smile. I answered each question in the order she requested, then stepped back and waited.

She brushed her hand in the air toward us. "Please stand aside while I talk with Eliezer." He came, and we turned away to give them privacy, but my heart stayed close.

Please...let me be the one chosen!

In but a moment, Eliezer came to me. Was I to be the first dismissed? Had I misread or made a mistake?

"Hagar, you have been chosen by our master's wife, Sarai, as her handmaiden. See that she is comfortable and watch with care that you may perceive her needs before she asks. You will begin your tasks in this moment. See to it now that she has a fan, kerchief, wrap, and skins of water."

I exhaled the sorrow of my past—and took my place in the royal cart beside my mistress.

At long last, the caravan moved forward.

We were leaving Egypt.

Memphis was all but a speck behind me and the pyramids soon disappeared from my sight.

The first few days of our journey through the desert of Sinai, Sarai was silent. I did not question or prod. I left her to her silent reflection, seeking only to serve her.

Then, one day, she began to talk in a low voice. Just above a whisper. Almost as though she spoke to herself—or perhaps to her God? Soon I realized she was retelling her story, all that had brought her to this place and time.

I spoke only to answer direct questions, which were few. But as I listened, her life with Abram unfolded. I heard how, years ago, God promised Abram would be the father of a great nation. That through him, all the nations of the earth would be blessed! Abram would have a son, and through him, God's Promise would be fulfilled.

And yet…Sarai had borne him no children.

As she spoke, grief and guilt overflowed her words. She closed her eyes against the truth, but tears escaped all the same. "I have been barren so many years…now I question if it is even possible for me to bear children."

I looked away as if I hadn't heard. Even though my mistress had experienced her God's deliverance in the House of Pharaoh, she had grown weary of this burden placed on her through a promise made to her husband.

I found her stories amazing. I absorbed every morsel. I could not believe how many times she had journeyed to different countries all because their God told Abram, "Go!"

A reverence for this unseen God of Abram grew within me. In Sarai's story, there were too many miracles that could not be accidental. For a moment, I lifted my eyes to search her face, and in the same instant lowered my gaze back to the ground.

Sarai must have seen my thoughts reflected in my eyes. She studied me. "Maiden, what are you thinking?"

"Is it your God's hand that guides you?"

"Abram says it is. And truly, each move has brought him closer to the fulfillment of God's Promise. Except…he still has no heir."

I wanted to comfort her—ask her to continue talking—to assure her all would be well. But it was not my place. I was a slave girl promoted to handmaiden, and Sarai? She was a princess and my owner. For me to offer comfort would be taking on a role beyond my station. And doing something beyond my station would be at best, unwise. At worse…

Fatal.

Groves of olive, oat, and palm trees appeared in the distance. Sarai roused from her midday nap and her eyes brightened. She sat up and stretched her arms. "Hebron is just ahead!"

The elements of desert travel and the stress of the time in Egypt had taken its toll. Sarai was tired. She was ready to be home. And so was I.

I leaned outside the cart to take in the scene before me. Abram's household and the herds of livestock gathered here, away from the vastness of Memphis stunned me. We were a massive village. With the spacious land here, everyone would have privacy.

Eliezer and his twelve assistants finalized their plans for the community. The hub would contain living quarters for Abram and Sarai, Eliezer, and twelve of his most loyal and trusted servants. I would be in the tent next to Sarai.

From there, housing positions were ranked by service importance. The slaves were placed on the outskirts of the camp.

Eliezer stood on a platform and pointed. "Our master's home will be here, near Abram's oak. This is his place of worship." I looked, but saw no monuments or idols, just the massive tree that spread out to extend over the plain stone altar. Sarai had told me of the importance of Abram's altar.

What a contrast to the gods of Egypt!

There, we worshipped gods created by man. But Abram worshipped the God that created man.

His altar was a place where God spoke. Oh, if He would ever speak to me....

I turned back to Eliezer to hear him finish. "Do not go near or interrupt Abram when you see him there, for this is his Holy Place." He spread out his plans and secured them with stones, then called his twelve officials to study—and implement—the plans.

There was a frenzied pace in the camp all during that first day, but by evening everything was in place. I marveled at the efficiency. And as I lay on my mat that night, I felt only peace.

I was home.

I settled into my new surroundings, relishing all the changes from our old life. The famine was over, the rains had come, and the hills and valleys abounded with flowers and new growth. The view was like a carpet spreading out before us.

Setting up housekeeping in Sarai's pavilion delighted me. She possessed beautiful curtains, wall hangings, and accessories collected from her many travels. Plush rugs covered the floor.

I pulled a beautiful vase from its packing.

"Maiden, place that in the far corner, where it will catch the morning light."

I did as my mistress bade me. Each unique item was unpacked with care and placed where she directed. Every treasure held a story, and I hoped I might hear them all. Temporary camps were all but forgotten now, for our dwellings were meant to be permanent.

I looked out to see hills surrounding the Hebron valley. Although the valley was void of great towers and temples, the landscape seemed fitting to our new way of life. Vineyards graced the land with the Grapes of Eschol. I had heard of these while in Egypt, and imagined their legend embellished. But now I saw firsthand—one cluster of the enormous grapes was a full load in my arms!

Soon, a pleasant pace was established and everyone worked in harmony. In Egypt, there were harsh and demanding taskmasters who had no consideration of need for rest. In Hebron, it was not so.

In Abram's world, there was no need for hurry. And in its place?

Peace.

Sarai trained me in the ways of Bedouin life. Each day brought a new lesson.

"Come, maiden," she would say. "Let me show you how to prepare these hearts of palm."

"Come, maiden, see how we season this meat."

"Come, maiden, observe how we mix these herbs."

I watched until I could prepare all her favorite foods from Canaan and Egypt.

Knowing her love of brilliant colors, I dyed fabrics and designed beautiful garments for her. Each day brought new wonders and beauty. And yet…

There were moments I observed Sarai deep in contemplation. At such times, a pervading gloom settled over her until she drifted to a dark place. That darkness overshadowed her kind disposition, and she withdrew.

She never told me what pained her so, but I knew. Was not a woman's worth measured by the number of male heirs she bore? Had not my mistress failed in this most coveted and natural act for a wife?

Though I would never have dared in our early days together, now I tried to bring comfort. Sometimes I combed and braided her hair. I commented on her beauty, always careful to keep my gaze lowered, submissive.

Today I wrapped a new scarf around her shoulders and held a silver tray for her to see her reflection. But nothing brought joy back to her countenance.

She suffered a silent grief. Her barrenness haunted her. And no matter how I longed to do so, there was no way I could ease the pain of her empty arms.

One night I entered Sarai's tent. "Do you need anything, My Lady, before I retire?"

"Yes, maiden, I am glad you came for there is something!"

I waited, eyes on the regal carpet at my feet. Never before had she spoken to me with this tone of…purpose.

"I want you to lie with my husband so you can conceive and bear a son for him, for me."

I could not help it—I looked at her. I could not speak. I would do anything for my mistress, but this? Many women gave their slaves to their husbands for concubines, but Sarai? Never. And Abram never sought any. They kept to each other. Never another.

How could this be her will?

Again, my mistress must have seen my thoughts, for her lips pressed together. Her eyes, which used to shine, now stared me into submission. She spoke no more. And I?

I lowered my eyes to the floor.

A slave.

"Yes, Mistress." I bowed, turned, and went to my tent.

I could not do it. Having intimate relations with an old man of eighty-six….

I could not!

I had not seen this side of Sarai before. One that showed no mercy, but rather used me to fulfill her dream and Abraham's promise. I was not stupid. I knew why Sarai chose me as her surrogate. Any child I bore would be hers. She owned me, so she would own my child. And the promise her God made to Abram would be fulfilled.

My hope lay with Abram. He would never stand for this plan, nor would his God. Abram went to his altar for instructions on every decision in his life. Surely, he would get his God's permission on Sarai's plan!

I could do nothing but wait.

Thoughts flowed through my mind. My son would be Abram's heir. My baby would fill Sarai empty arms. But where would I be in all of this? Would my mistress let me see my child at all? Would I be a wet nurse, but nothing more, to my own child?

Sarai would raise him. Would he ever be allowed to know me as his mother? How many children might I bear Abram? And how long would it take before I bore the first? What if the child were a girl? Would she die for my failure to produce a son?

Was this my destiny? To be used, first by Sarai and then Abram?

A sound at the tent doorway brought me to my feet. Abram entered, and I knelt before him. Hoping, begging Abram's God for Abram to release me. Instead…

Abram reached for my hand.

Abram came to my tent often. Sarah became more abrupt with me, taking her ambivalence out on me, treating me with contempt and distain. I had seen how the women in the harems of Egypt were at each other's throats. How they screeched over whom the pharaoh loved best. And now Sarai became one of those self-focused, mean-spirited shrews. I grew weary of her treatment and for the first time, disliked being around her.

One evening, after a long day, I settled into my bed, exhausted. I knew my monthly cycle would begin the next day, giving me two weeks of Abram's absence in my bed. Perhaps Sarai would stop staring at my stomach for a sign.

Eight days passed, then sixteen—and I knew. I would indeed bear a child. I was both startled and excited. Startled because I knew nothing about childbirth, yet excited because I wouldn't have to sleep with Abram again. The truth could be told now.

Everything changed. No longer was I being used. Instead, I was now Prince Abram's vessel, destined to bear his child. And that's when I realized it.

The servant had done something her mistress had not. No, more than that.

Something her mistress *could not.*

I came into Sarai presence, and when she looked at me, I met her gaze—and held it. Sarai started, and then frowned.

"Maiden, your gaze is elevated this day."

Her tone made it clear she was not pleased with my manner, but for the first time, I did not care.

Her frown deepened. "What has happened to bring about this… change?"

Let her be sarcastic. Let her look down on me. She was no longer my mistress, not in my heart. For I had done what she could not. I did not hide my smile. "Mistress"—I gave her sarcasm for sarcasm, and then uttered the words that would defeat her—"I'm pregnant."

Sarai stiffened. "Indeed? Then you have served the purpose for which I chose you."

I dared not defy her further and so lowered my gaze. But still I smiled.

"Leave me."

I was only too happy to do so. I turned, my back straight, my head high, and walked with the slow, easy pace of a woman who knows she has gained new position. I was elevated beyond the status of a slave. I bore my master's child! His heir! I would be under Abram's covering and care.

Much would come to me now. Me, Hagar, the invisible girl from Egypt. Nothing could harm me because Abram was the prince, the head of this great village. And I was the mother of his child!

Sarai had her beauty, but I?

I had Abram's child.

That night, in the tent next to mine, I heard Sarai tell Abram my news. From the way she was screaming, the whole camp probably heard as well.

"This is all your fault! I put my servant into your arms and now she treats me with contempt."

I delighted in hearing her complaint. But wait…there was more. Abram spoke.

"She is your maidservant."

What? I crept closer, certain I had heard wrong. But no, he said it again.

And worse.

"This woman is your maidservant, Sarai. If you do not like her words or actions, then do with her as you please."

How could this be? How could he say such a thing? Wouldn't I be under his covering of protection because of his child? I closed my eyes. Listened.

There was only silence.

Abram, the father of my child, did nothing to redeem me.

The truth settled in. I was alone.

And I would suffer the wrath of Sarai.

Life became unbearable as Sarai returned with vengeance the contempt I had so foolishly shown her.

Oh, that I had not shown her the ugly face of my pride! Why did I do it? How could I have believed I was anything more than a slave? Anything more than…

Property.

Now I was paying. I was concerned for the life within me more than my own life. I had to escape the intolerable torment she inflicted. There was only one answer.

I ran away.

I purposed to return to Egypt. Once there, I would go where no one knew me. For if I did not, I would be put on the trading block. Sold to another master. Separated from my child.

No, that would not happen. I would find a place where I could raise my child. I would love this baby and be loved in return. That is, if I could find my way back. Which was far more difficult than I ever imagined.

After two full days of travel, I sat, exhausted, hungry, and thirsty. Alone in the wilderness, scared, and wild with fear, questions crowded my mind.

How could I have run with no plan?

Would we be devoured by wild beasts? Was I to starve or die of thirst? Which would kill me first—the desert sun or the frigid nights?

With each new question, hope evaporated like the sweat from my drying, cracking skin. Only a miracle would save me now.

I wept, but there was no moisture within me for tears. And then…

"Hagar."

I froze. The hairs on my arms raised, and chills traveled down my back.

"Hagar."

Who would call my name out here in this desolate place where I prepared to die?

The voice came again, filled with love and tenderness. "Hagar, servant of Sarai, where have you come from, and where are you going?"

And then I knew. This was the voice of Abram's God…of the Lord God….

And He knew my name!

I had observed Abram praying to his God at the altar under the great oak tree. I heard him acknowledge promises that God had made to him. Abram affirmed that he would forever believe God's promises. Now, his God spoke to me!

What God would ever call out to me, a lowly servant? I trembled as I answered. "I am fleeing from the presence of my mistress, Sarai."

"Go back to your mistress and submit to her authority."

For all that the words were not what I wanted to hear, they were spoken with such love I could not resist. But the Lord God's next words lifted my grieving heart.

"I will multiply your descendants in abundance, so that they shall not be counted for the multitude."

I received the promise, embraced it. I believed in Abram's God—my God—and peace flooded me.

God was not finished. "You are now pregnant and will give birth to a son. You are to name him Ishmael, for God hears—the Lord has heard your cry of distress."

I dropped to my knees and bowed my head. I mattered to God! I was not invisible.

My Creator acknowledged me—heard me.

"This son of yours will be a wild man, as untamed as a wild donkey! He will raise his fist against everyone, and everyone will be against him. Yes, he will live in open hostility against all his relatives."

I tried to take it all in, but what did it mean? Would my son break free of slavery in his lifetime and fight to defend his birthright? I prayed this was so, for it would mean I was free as well. His life would be hard. Hard as mine. But with a blessing from the God of Abram…

"Because the Lord has heard your affliction—"

There was more? From my knees, I cried out. I wanted to give Him a name I never knew before: "El Roi…The God who sees me." Tears flooded my face. God saw me, and spoke my name!

I knelt. This place would be my altar.

The sense of God's presence wrapped around me like a warm blanket. No matter if I went back to be tortured by Sarai. The God above all gods knew I existed and He treasured me.

He was my Father.

With God's assurance inside, I would return to Abram and Sarai.

But now I had a plan. Or rather, God had one for me. A plan to bless me, guide me, and give me hope for the future. Now, armed with God's blessing, I could face whatever was before me.

I retraced the steps that led me here, knowing each one brought me closer to submitting to Sarai's authority.

I arrived the evening of the fourth day. I knew what I should—rather, must,—say. I must ask for forgiveness. Then wait to see if she would permit me to take my place again under her direction. I would do whatever it took to redeem myself and leave the result with God…for since my wilderness experience…I was under a higher authority.

The servants saw me in the distance and came to me. "We have told Sarai of your return, and she asks that you wait here."

I waited. My future rested in her hands. She must have been relieved when I ran away. Now, my return would bring more pain to Sarai. Even if she refused me, I had done what the Angel of the LORD directed. He would provide.

Soon Sarai walked to the door of her tent and motioned me inside. She sat. I stood in silence, waiting. It was not my place to speak first. Sarai looked not at me, but past me. As though building courage to speak.

At last, she moved her eyes to meet mine, and when she spoke, it was with the voice of a friend. "Are you well, Hagar?"

Hagar? Not maiden? Sarai called me by my name!

"I am well, Mistress, but my spirit is troubled, for I flaunted the joy of my pregnancy before you. I relished in shaming you. For this, I am truly sorry. I was wrong. I beg your forgiveness."

"Welcome home, Hagar."

Just like that? I was received, restored? From what I saw on Sarai's face…it was so. And her next words confirmed it.

"Go, refresh yourself, take nourishment, and rest from your journey." With a gentle motion of her hand, she dismissed me.

I turned to leave, my heart light within me.

So this was how it felt to be forgiven.

Free.

Although fear still tempted, I was comforted by God's promise and guidance. I vowed to walk with a more humble spirit before my master and mistress.

Sarai received me, but she spent more time alone, not requesting my service. I understood. It would be difficult for her in the months ahead. I tried to live in the shadows, not make it harder on Sarai than it was.

One day, while I was at the well, Abram approached and sat beside me. "I know the time of the birth is nigh. Are you well?"

"I am well. It won't be long." I studied his face. "I found your God in the wilderness, when I ran away."

He listened.

"He called me by name and gave me a promise of blessing, descendants beyond number. He said this son is called Ishmael."

Abram caught his breath. "A son, Ishmael…God hears!"

He extended his hand and drew me near, and placed his hand on my stomach. The baby kicked hard. Abram's eyes brightened and he bent down, pressing his ear to hear. He lifted his head. There were tears in his eyes. "My son kicked and I heard his heartbeat!"

This was the first time I had experienced my master's love and attachment to my child—or his fondness for me. I closed my eyes and cherished the moment.

When I opened my eyes, I saw Sarai in the distance. She turned, but not before I saw the pain this brought. My heart ached that she had seen that tender moment.

In the early morning, I awakened to sharp, intense pain.

My son would be born this day.

I called the handmaiden Abram gave me, telling her to bring the midwife. Within moments, they both were at my side. At each unbearable stab, the tender touch of their care soothed me.

At last, I heard the cry of my newborn. The midwife placed my son in my arms, and I wept. It was exactly as God had promised.

Abram rushed in at the cry of the babe. He took him from my arms and raised him above his head. "My God, my God, Thou hast not forsaken me. He shall take the name you gave him, Ishmael."

Abram was so proud of his son! He held him close and told him about God's promises and the journey that lead us all to that moment.

My baby suckled at my breast and wrapped his tiny hand around my little finger. Such strength for one so small.

As the days passed, Sarai was on the outside looking in. She could not be pleased with the outcome of her plan. She never claimed my child as her own. I don't know if Abram forbade her, if God prevented her, or perhaps she didn't want him after all. Whatever the reason, one fact rang in my heart.

He was my son.

Abram became a true father. He spent much time teaching Ishmael about his God, educating, and training him in survival and trade skills. My little son watched and learned, unaware he was being taught by a master.

But I knew. And I thanked El Roi for all we were given. And I prayed that all our days would be filled with this calm and peace.

When Ishmael was thirteen, Abram told me that God spoke to him again. He changed Abram's name to Abraham, meaning Father of Nations. He said God also had given Sarai the new name of Sarah, Mother of Nations.

So…was the promise still there? That Sarai—no, Sarah—would bear a child? How could that be? Sarah was going on ninety!

But it wasn't long before I watched another miracle, the greatest miracle of God! Sarah was pregnant! What joy sprang through the camp. Everyone was thrilled. How marvelous was our God. Life sprang forth from a dead womb as Sarah bore a son. They named him Isaac—laughter.

I saw God and His power at work in all our lives.

At last, Sarah had her son. Heaven and earth could not contain her joy. A lifetime of worry and sadness were washed away from her.

As was the fear that had followed me for so long. We each had a son. Our lives were complete.

When Isaac was weaned, Abraham planned a great celebration. The baby had become a three-year-old who talked and laughed with his family. On that day of joy, Sarah and I observed something troubling: Ishmael teased and taunted Isaac. I was concerned, but Sarah?

She was enraged.

In that moment, the old fear that had haunted me for so long returned, for I did not know what Sarah's rage would bring.

That evening as I walked near Abraham's altar, I heard him crying out to his God.

"What should I do? Sarah has demanded me to get rid of Hagar and my son."

Get rid of us? I gasped as fear ran through me. El Roi, will You let this happen?

"She announced to me that Isaac would never share my inheritance with Ishmael."

The voice that answered Abraham was the same voice I heard in the wilderness.

"Do not be upset over the boy and your servant. Do whatever Sarah tells you, for Isaac is the son through whom your descendants will be counted. But I will also make a nation of the descendants of Hagar's son, because he is your son, too."

I went to my tent, still fearful but comforted. God saw us and He would not abandon us.

The next morning, Abraham came to us before dawn. His sadness pierced me as he told us of Sarah's distress. "I went to seek God at my altar and He told me to do as Sarah asked. Hagar, I am sorry but you and Ishmael must leave. Now."

I saw the pain in Abraham, for he loved his son. I had grown to love Abraham for loving our son. But this? I had no answer. I had not expected to leave my home so quickly or permanently.

Abraham prayed for us, and shared what the Lord God promised him. "He told me, 'And as for Ishmael, I have heard thee: Behold, I have blessed him, and will make him fruitful, and will multiply him exceedingly; twelve princes shall he beget, and I will make him a great nation.'"

Another promise for Ishmael! God was watching over us.

With tears in his eyes, he gave us bread and water for the journey… and sent us away. On our journey to—we knew not where.

We started in the direction where Abraham trained Ishmael. We did not want to leave, and yet we were happy at the thought of our freedom.

We talked of what our future might be like away from Abraham and Sarah. Ishmael talked about how he would take care of me—my son had a man's protective heart.

We wandered in the wilderness of Beersheba for five days and nights. It was so hot! We drank all our water in the first three days, but I was not worried. We would find water along the way. We both knew how to travel, how to survive. And yet, as the days wore on, there was no water to be found. None of our knowledge would help us survive without the most important element: water.

I was thirsty and weak. I grew to detest this hot, dry, desolate place. There was not a cloud in the sky. The blistering sun beat down, and there was no place to seek shelter from the brutal elements of the desert. No trees, only a few bushes. We stumbled, and fell…and Ishmael could not rise.

My son cried out, death on his lips. "Mother…can't go…farther." His lips were cracked and his face scorched. The redness had turned to blisters. "Mother, Mother, I am thirsty…."

His words, his pain, led me to despair. "Forgive me El Roi, I am losing hope. My faith is fading."

I could no longer endure Ishmael's pleas for help. Every time he cried out, I was torn apart by a terrible grief. I saw a tree in the distance, moved him under it, and walked a little way away so I could not hear his dying cries. He could not last much longer.

I sat down. At that moment, I remembered what God had promised me all those years ago in my wilderness journey. I cried out to the God Who Sees Me and hears my cry. "Where is the God of Abraham? Why have You deserted me? I trusted Your promise. I believed in You. We need You now."

And then His voice was there, around me, filling me. Within me.

"Hagar, what's wrong? Do not be afraid! I have heard the boy crying as he lies there. Go to him and comfort him, for I will make a great nation from his descendants."

God opened my eyes, and I saw a well of water! Oh, how I ached that I had doubted Him even for a moment. My soul repented for doubting the God who spoke to me when I needed Him most.

I grabbed the skins, hurried to the well, and filled them with water! Cool, refreshing, and marvelous water! I walked to my son and splashed water all over his body, cooling and reviving him. I gave him a long drink, and as Ishmael's eyes met mine, I knew we would survive.

We were in the shelter of God's love. We need never fear again.

God would provide.

We began our new life together with the promises of God to guide and direct us to our destinies.

The future lay ahead of us. We were no longer Abraham's property.

We were free.

When Abraham released us from his care, I was no longer a bondservant. And, at the age of seventeen, Ishmael was a free man. When a master released his servant, it signified freedom, but forbade claim to any inheritance from his master. The Lord's covenant also made it clear that Ishmael was not to inherit Abraham's house. Isaac would be the sole instrument of the covenant.

And so we lived in the wilderness, where Ishmael became an excellent hunter. We built a home and God provided wild berries, nuts, and honey from the vines and trees. In time, we were able to trade meat and skins to traders for items we needed in Paran.

The blessing of God was upon Ishmael as He had promised. Everything my son did prospered. When the time was right, we made the journey to find a wife for him from Egypt. We settled in the Desert of Paran, where Ishmael had twelve sons who became princes throughout the twelve regions of land from Assyria to the border of Egypt.

I reflected on God's promise to me here in the wilderness of my wonderings. I accepted my destiny, which was tied to His promise, and I would not doubt. I would also be the mother of a great nation because God spoke it. I chose to trust Him.

When Abraham died, my son and his brother met after being separated for many years. Isaac, with his hundreds of household slaves, and Ishmael, with his wild troops and half-savage bands, both standing out among their people as Bedouin Princes, gathered before the cave of Machpelah.

There in the midst of the Hittites, they paid their last duties to their father, who was called the "Father of the Faithful." Both princes rightly claimed Abraham as the father and founder of their people.

And yet, as they stood there, I knew. The enmity was still there. If anything, it was deeper than ever. My son, my Ishmael, was not at peace with his brother.

Perhaps he never would be.

Despair touched my mother's heart. What grief I felt that these two sons of Abraham were always in conflict.

But I knew the truth. Through Abraham's seed, through both Isaac and Ishmael, there was birthed a beginning of two great nations. God's promise to Abraham, that through him all the nations of the earth would be blessed, was coming true. My son was part of this promise.

As was I.

For the times in my life when I was lost, when I felt I was without hope, God was there to rescue me. I came to trust Him with both the good and the bad of my life. For He was El Roi, the God Who Sees Me.

For me.

For my son.

And for all who came after us.

Read Hagar's story in Genesis 16-21

CHAPTER 4
Rebekah

AS I SAT upon the magnificent camel, moving through the desert like a ship gliding across the sea, I could not keep from looking at the spectacular gold, gems, and pearls that adorned me. A treasure befitting a royal princess. My mind raced at what awaited me. I was leaving all that I knew, all that was dear to me, and heading toward a new life, in a new country. Even more important...

To a new destiny.

How did this happen to me?

One moment I was at the well, drawing water, and the next...seated atop a camel, surrounded by a compliment of maidens to look after me, and guards dressed in dark Bedouin tunics with sashes and full headdress. Swords in leather scabbards hung at their side. They too were mounted on camels. Ten in a row. But at my side and leading the splendid caravan was the majestic Eliezer, Abraham's trusted servant.

I turned around. All I knew shrank from my sight as my camel plied the desert sands, carrying me farther and farther away. My future in the distant land of Canaan, some four hundred miles away, overwhelmed my thoughts. I was on my way to marry a man I had never met.

And only heard about yesterday....

Yesterday, as the only daughter of Laban and the water bearer for my family, I made my way to the well, just outside the village of Haran, in Mesopotamia. The waters from this well had supported our village for more than the four generations, since my family settled here with my great grandfather Terah.

Travelers stopped to rest under the shelter of the oak trees and waited for permission to drink from the well. A city grew, flourished because of it. The unending need for its life giving provision drew everyone. The news center of Haran, a place to draw water, and a meeting place for all, one could know everything happening in the city and, much more.

I'd made the journey a thousand times in my youth—since the day I was strong enough to carry the earthen vessel. I knew the path well but dared not close my eyes for a moment—else I might miss seeing friends, relatives, or interesting travelers. Some spoke strange languages, wore different clothing: some exotic, some magnificent, and some ordinary. These people, all going or coming to where all were drawn…with the same need—water. We were all equal…at the well.

This chore had always been my favorite part of my day. It awakened the dreamer within for as I stepped outside, even yesterday, I knew…

It *could* be the day.

The day my life would change. The day my dreams would come true. For the something—Someone—had planted, deep in my heart, a sure knowledge that my path would not end where it began. No, I was meant for something…

More.

Did the well hold the key?

A special treat awaited. There were strangers gathered at the well. As I drew near, I saw an old man sitting, so regal with his snow-white hair and long, full beard. He wore fine garments and held a handsome carved cane. His servant guards surrounded him. Their very manner exuded importance. A host of camels knelt by the wayside, resting. Some packed high with bundles and boxes. Some wore ornaments adorned with silver regalia.

Such an impressive gathering! I looked around. If I hurried, I would be the first to welcome them.

The stranger's face looked into the heavens, as if praying. I did not want to disturb him so I took the steps down to the water and filled my pitcher. As I returned, the stranger spoke. "Maiden, may I have a drink from your pitcher?"

Excited, I turned, looking into his piercing eyes. I smiled. "Yes, My Lord." I lowered my vessel from my shoulder, giving him water.

Something within prompted me to ask. "Sir, may I bring water for your servants and animals too?" This surprised me for as I spoke those words, my heart sensed something more….

The minute the words left my lips, a mysterious transformation overtook the man. His eyes brightened, and a magnificent smile adorned his face.

He inclined his head to me and raised his hand. "This is a blessing far beyond what you realize Maiden. I am humbled by your kind act of service to me, a stranger among you."

His blessing washed over me, warming me.

I emptied my pitcher into the trough as I looked to see eight, nine, ten camels, all thirsty.

I almost danced down to the well. How could this be one of the greatest gifts he had ever received?

I poured many pitchers of water, first for the servants and then filling the troughs until every camel was satisfied. Now I had another story to add to my memories here.

When I returned with the water for our home, the man called out to me. "Maiden, come here please. I want to give you something for your kindness."

From his pouch, he first handed me a gold ring. How it shone in the sunlight! Then he reached into the bag again, brought up two heavy gold bracelets, and placed one on each of my wrists.

Never had I been adorned with such beautiful things, even in my dreams!

I stared at my new gifts, and for a moment, my tongue was silent. I looked into the man's eyes when I found my voice. "Thank you, My Lord."

He squinted as he studied my face. I expected him to say, "You are welcome." But he continued to search me, almost looking inside…"Whose daughter are you?"

"I am the daughter of Bethuel, and my grandparents are Nahor and Milcah."

This seemed to be the very answer he expected for he asked yet another question. "Tell me, maiden, would your father have room to put us up for the night?"

The very thought of having guests lifted my soul. "Yes, he can! We have plenty of food and straw for your camels."

The man fell to his knees, bowing his head low. "Praise the Lord, the God of my master, Abraham, The Lord has shown unfailing love and faithfulness to my master, for He has led me straight to my master's relatives."

Abraham? I knew of him. He was my grandfather's brother, my great uncle! My family would be very excited.

"Permit me to go ahead and tell my family. The men will come at once to bring you to our home."

He inclined his head. I ran all the way home, leaving my vessel there. I burst into the room. "We have many guests for the night!"

I told my family all that had happened. At once, my brother Laban eyed my new jewelry and, with a twinkle in his eye, announced he would be happy to run to the well and bring the servants of Abraham, to our home.

Laban returned with the travelers and it was Laban, not our servants, who unloaded the camels, fed, and gave straw bedding for the animals. He set out water for the man and camel drivers to wash their feet.

As I watched my brother work, he did not look weary in the least. No, the smile on his face told me the blessings were just beginning!

Mother and I set out the evening meal.

The man I'd spoken with came inside with Father and Laban. His bearing still regal, adding an air of importance to our home. His servants stood behind him, waiting.

As Mother announced the meal, the man started. "I'm sorry but I cannot eat until I tell you the purpose of my visit."

My brother's response was immediate. "All right, then tell us!"

We gathered around the man, as he spoke. "My name is Eliezer. I am the servant of your relative Abraham, a prince in his country who has sheep, cattle, silver, gold, maidservants, and men servants in Hebron."

Father nodded. "We know very well of Abraham, who left our family here to follow his God to Canaan."

At the man's mention of his wealthy master, Laban's eyes lit up. He leaned in closer as Eliezer continued.

"My master will pass all this great wealth to his son, Isaac."

Again, Laban drew close. I could guess at the question in his mind: "So where do we fit in to this great wealth?"

"My master's wife, Sarah, bore this son to Abraham in his old age. He was her only son. She has died and Abraham made me take an oath saying, 'Do not allow my son to marry one of these local Canaanite women. Go instead to my father's house, to my relatives, and find a suitable wife there for my son.'"

A wife? Could it be…?

Was I to become part of this story? Now my ears listened intently.

"But, I said to my master, 'What if I can't find a young woman who is willing to go back with me?' He responded, "The Lord, in whose presence I have lived, will send His angel with you and will make your mission successful. Yes, you must find a wife for my son from among my relatives, from my father Terah's family. Then you will have fulfilled your obligation. But, if you go to my relatives and they refuse to let her go with you, you will be free from my oath."

"So today when I arrived at the well, I prayed this prayer: 'O LORD God of my master, Abraham, please give me success on this mission. See, I am standing here beside this spring, and the young women of the town are coming out to draw water. This is my request. I will ask one of them, 'Please give me a drink from your jug.' If she says, 'Yes, have a drink, and I will water your camels too'—let her be the one you have selected as Isaac's wife. This is how I will know that you have shown unfailing love to my master.'"

My heart beat faster and faster.

I had watered his camels!

Eliezer continued. "Before I finished praying in my heart, I saw Rebekah coming out with her water jug on her shoulder."

At the thought of this, my destiny was shaped somehow, this very day, this very moment. As he recounted our conversation, I shook with excitement. It was really happening! My dream unfolding before me, not because Father and Laban had made it happen, but…

Because the Lord God of Abraham did so!

Eliezer looked from my brother to my father. "Because of the answer to my prayer, I ask that you permit your daughter Rebekah to accompany me back to my master's son and become his wife."

So there, he had said it.

So many reactions my family had to his question! Laban looked as though he would explode if someone didn't respond quickly, but Father remained silent, lost in thought. Mother hurried to stand by me and placed her hand on my shoulder.

As for my reaction? I almost fainted!

Father and Laban both spoke. One adding a sentence and the other the next.

"The Lord has obviously brought you here, so there is nothing else we can say."

"Here is Rebekah—we will not stand in the way of God." And then, "Yes, let her be the wife of your master's son."

Though it was the hardest thing I've ever done, I kept silent, as did mother. She squeezed my shoulder.

Eliezer spoke no more, but bowed down to the ground and worshiped the Lord, in our front room.

I could not take it all in, all my ears had heard. The servants were quiet, waiting, as their master continued to pray. But I would not know the details about my future until this man spoke again.

At last, Eliezer rose and motioned his servants to follow him outside, where his camels rested. How strange. Were they going to return to Canaan? Should I follow them?

I turned to look to my mother, who gave a nervous smile. Then I faced my brother, who strained his neck to see what Eliezer was doing. Finally, I searched my father's eyes. What I saw there was clear. We could do nothing but wait for the messenger to return.

True, I was old enough to be married, but we had never spoken of it. Was I now engaged to someone from another land? A land—and a man—I had never laid eyes on?

Eliezer and his men returned, carrying many bundles. "I have brought gifts for you from my master."

He looked at me. I moved to his side.

"Rebekah, for you."

I stared. He handed me a cedar box with gold bands encircling the edges. It was heavy.

"Rebekah, this is a gift worthy of the wife of Isaac, my master's son. Please open the box and see what my master has provided for you."

He handed me a key.

I opened the lid and looked inside. What I saw took my breath away—rings, bracelets, gold chains, earrings, pearls, and sparkling gemstones.

A prince's ransom...for me.

Feeling faint, I sat on the bench to compose myself. I cradled the box. Could I be this valuable to anyone?

The gifts continued. He gave me beautiful garments, so many, I was embarrassed for I had yet to own more than a few dresses, let alone precious ones like these. All of a sudden, I realized he was adorning the bride for Isaac!

He gave many gifts to my brother Laban, who could not hide his delight. In fact, my brother was quite overcome, having a hard time suppressing his pleasure.

I smiled as Eliezer adorned my mother with lovely jewelry and gave her many exquisite items of gold, silver, and two fine garments. She tried one on and emerged looking every bit a member of royalty. Dressed like this, she was more beautiful than I had ever seen her.

As I gazed on all this bounty...I knew. All these treasures were the bride-price for me!

I was, indeed...

Betrothed.

I remembered my dreams for a husband yet never dreamed he would be one I had never seen.

At last, we reclined for our meal. But who could sit still, let alone eat, after such magnificent treasures given? I kept looking at my jewels and then to my mother. We shared our joy without words.

When we finished eating, Eliezer said he and his men were tired, so Laban showed them where they could sleep.

Laban and father came back to join mother and me. Father said, "Rebekah, I did not have to labor in finding a suitable husband for you. And yet one has found you just the same."

When I finally lay down, I pondered the things that would not happen here again: sleeping in the bed of my youth, eating with my family, kissing my mother goodnight…visiting friends, and bringing water from the well. These thoughts brought sadness but joy replaced them with great anticipation for my new life.

Would I ever return? If I did, would it have been so long since I'd seen them that I wouldn't even recognize my own mother and father? Would there be a well of this magnitude in Hebron?

Most of all, I thought about Isaac.

When Isaac gazed at me for the first time, would he be pleased?

Morning came at last. I dressed quickly. I heard Eliezer's voice.

"Please let us return to my master today."

"But we want Rebekah to stay with us at least ten days," Laban said. "Then she can go."

Ten more days? Ten more days…I did not want to stay another moment while my happy future waited for me in Canaan!

Do not disappoint me Eliezer! Don't give in.

His response was firm. "Don't delay me. The Lord has made my mission successful. Now send me back so I can present Rebekah to my master's son."

Yes! I almost said it aloud, which would give away my place behind the curtain.

"Well"—clearly, my brother was hesitant. "We'll ask Rebekah what she thinks."

What was he thinking? Of course, I would say yes!

"Rebekah, are you willing to go with this man?"

I stepped from behind the curtain, hesitating as a pretense, pondering the question. Last night everyone had been overjoyed at the promise for me, now I could not read their faces. So…

It was up to me?

Trying to conceal my excitement, the words betrayed my pause and slipped out—a little louder than I planned.

"I will go!"

I gathered my treasures and the servants loaded them on the camels. Soon I was ready. I looked at my family, knowing they were sad at my departure but excited that this blessing came to me.

My family put their arms around me cradling me in their circle. They blessed me. "Our sister, may you become the mother of many millions! May your descendants be strong and conquer the cities of their enemies."

I bade them farewell. I was leaving my homeland for perhaps forever. Tears fell as I turned toward Eliezer.

I looked to the long line of camels ready for their journey home. Little had I known when I carried water for them that the treasures they bore were for me and that they would carry me to the man who would fulfill my dreams.

Eliezer's servants led me to my camel. It was grand, decorated in such finery. The animal wore ornaments, tassels, a silver harness, and a beautiful leather saddle.

I waited as Eliezer instructed his servants but my heart had already started its journey.

We stopped at the well. Was it only yesterday I met Eliezer here? I was leaving the very place that brought me such happiness through the years and now bestowed the promise of my happy future. I hoped my family would retell this story many times.

The servants drew water. Sadness gripped me. I placed my hand on my heart and thanked the Lord God for what He had done for me here at the well. My heart was full as were my eyes.

The city of Haran was all but behind me.

I was on my way to a new land, a new home, a new life.

And a new well.

During our journey, Eliezer spent many hours telling of his history with Abraham and Isaac. "I have worked since my childhood for this family and have come to care for them as my own kindred."

"Abraham is blessed to have a servant like you, Eliezer."

"God promised Abraham that through him, all the nations of the earth would be blessed and his descendants would be as numerous as the sand of the seashore. God has spoken to my master many times. They are friends. He has provided you for Isaac, and you are now a part of God's promise. Through you, Isaac will continue the line of Abraham to the next generation and beyond."

Eliezer paused, and his voice lowered. "Isaac grieves his mother's death. He is almost forty and now you, God's chosen one, will bring him joy and fulfillment. You will turn his heart from mourning to laughter, from sadness to joy. You are the companion he needs. And God, through answering my prayer has confirmed all this. This is right for you and it is right for Isaac. You need not worry, you need not fear. Isaac is perfect for you and you for him. "

"Eliezer, through your words, your God is becoming real to me and as the Lord wills, so will I be."

From all Eliezer told me, I knew Isaac was a devoted, loyal, and sensitive man who honored his parents and loved his God. I could listen for hours as Eliezer talked about the family that would soon be mine. They had experienced many miracles and adventures.

I asked again. "Do you think Isaac will be pleased with me?"

"Your heart and your beauty will overwhelm him."

"Is he tall?"

"As a cypress tree."

"Is he handsome?"

"As handsome as his mother was beautiful."

Who among us had not heard of Sarah's profound beauty?

And yet, I couldn't help it. More questions tumbled out. "Is he strong?"

Eliezer laughed. "Isaac is all this and more. You will be well pleased."

"You are sure?"

"Rebekah, this is ordained in heaven and blessed by the Lord God! The outcome of this marriage will be more than you ever dreamed."

"Then it would be wondrous indeed!"

Each day, as I sat atop my camel, I pictured him, this Isaac, who would be my husband, provider, protector, and father of my children. I pictured him with broad shoulders and strong arms. Each night, I plied Eliezer with more questions. Where would we live? What would I do? He never seemed to tire of answering.

And as I dreamed, the days flew by.

One day, it happened.

We approached Negev, the desert surrounding Hebron. We would arrive at my new home within the day.

Eliezer pointed out tents and awnings, miniature dots on the horizon that were more visible as we drew near Abraham and Isaac's homeland.

There was a man walking in the fields of grain. As our caravan approached, something about him…stirred me. I couldn't take my eyes off him. My heart leapt within me. I tried to remain calm, but my excitement spilled over. "Who is that man?"

Eliezer smiled. "It is Isaac. He walks in the fields each evening to worship, pray to God, and meditate."

I could not contain my excitement. I dismounted with the help of a servant. As I waited for Eliezer's instructions, I put on my wedding veil. I was more than ready to meet Isaac.

My husband!

Eliezer walked with me, calling out to Isaac as we drew near. "Master, your father asked me to bring you a wife from his homeland and this is the one God has picked for you. With my task accomplished, here is the beautiful Rebekah."

I did not think Isaac heard Eliezer, and yet he ran toward us. Oh, Eliezer had been conservative. Isaac was a man of princely stature. His muscles bulged even through his tunic. He was a spectacle for my eyes. He *was* tall! He had curly ebony hair and a full beard, trimmed to perfection. His skin was tanned and his teeth white as goat's milk. He moved toward me with grace. Our eyes locked. He stared through my veil, searching….

Eliezer tried again. "Isaac, this is Rebekah!"

This, Isaac heard. He looked at his father's servant, and then to me. "The beautiful and lovely Rebekah is truly of the Lord. I could not be more pleased."

The response of a man devoted to his God filled me. I turned to smile at Eliezer, but the servant was walking away. His face to the wind as his purple tunic flowed and his blessing came to us on the breeze. With one hand in the air and his eyes toward heaven, "God bless you, keep you, make His face to shine on you, and be gracious to you. The Lord lift up His countenance upon you and give you peace…."

He was gone.

Isaac looked into my eyes and took my hands. The feel of his strong hands cradling mine enveloped me. I felt so…

Nervous.

My heart trembled, as did Isaac's hands.

Isaac raised my veil, looked into my eyes, and kissed me.

"Rebekah, my Rebekah, you are more than beautiful. I have waited my whole life for one such as you. I know this is of God, for I loved you the moment I saw you. I need no other. I will love and cherish you all the days of my life."

His words rang with truth and conviction. I responded without hesitation: "And I, you!"

So this was my destiny, more than I ever dreamed, even on my best days. Isaac led me to his mother's tent. I did not hesitate. The well had delivered more than water to me. To us.

The grieving for his mother ended, never to return.

After our wedding week, Isaac took me to Abraham. "Father, this is my wife Rebekah."

Abraham paused, looking straight into my eyes.

"Isaac, Eliezer's words did not prepare me for this. I am near speechless. Your Rebekah's beauty rivals that of your mother."

I moved closer. He took my hands and kissed my cheeks. "God has provided a daughter-in-law for me. I am well pleased." He stood as he placed his hand on my head. "May God bless you and continue to bless you with love, children, and His guidance as He has guided me. Welcome to our family, my daughter."

I explored their vast encampment. I walked among the peoples. I saw women preparing food outside their tents: breads, meats, stews, and vegetables. The blend of aromas tantalized my senses, inciting me to linger. Such a sense of community here. A place of joy and peace just as Eliezer had said. In the shadow of Abraham and Isaac, the people rested for both Abraham and Isaac were at rest in the shadow of their God.

Some days I rode my camel through the fields, my hair blowing in the wind, the smell of the grass, the blossoms on the trees, their fragrance floating in the air. I felt free. Children of all ages played. I gazed as they ran, laughing, chasing goats, sheep, and each other.

Then it dawned on me.

I was ready to be a mother.

I walked from the tent Isaac and I had shared for the past five years. I surveyed those bustling around me. How their lives had changed, servants I had known all these years. Many maidens had married, and I watched as one of them drew her small one close, kissed his cheek, and brushed his hair out of his dark round eyes. The smile on her face, the pride in her eyes…was what awaited me.

My dreams of a husband, of a home, and a new life had all come true. And yet, to fulfill my perfect dream, I needed a child.

Even as the grief struck me again, I felt strong arms circle me from behind.

"Are you well this morning, my wife?"

I leaned back, resting my head against my husband's powerful chest. "It has been five years, Isaac. Look at all these women, all their children. Why have I not known this blessing from the Lord God?"

"My love, do not worry for this is in God's hands. Because of His promise to my father, I know that in His time, you will bear children. Be patient. My own mother waited many years past childbearing age before I was born. We will not lose heart. We will trust God for His promises fail not. In His time, Rebekah, I know beyond any doubt that you will bear an heir."

And so I waited…ten, fifteen, and going on twenty years. Isaac's words kept assuring me to have faith, to trust God but still I grieved at being denied a child and labeled barren.

I rested in the fact that Isaac took no handmaiden, concubine, or second wife. I accounted his patience to his faith. Oh that I could believe and be content. His strong faith and patience could not cover my frustration. I could no longer be quieted. I wailed. "Isaac, how am I to continue your father's lineage if I cannot bear a child?"

He placed his large, strong hand on my head. His fingers reaching to my ears. "Almighty God of my father, hear my plea and grant Rebekah's dream to be a mother. Give us a child, Holy God, but more than that, let her trust You as I do. Take this burden from her. Open her heart and her womb. Allow Rebekah the joy of Your promise fulfilled."

In that moment, I opened my heart to the promise of Isaac's God, accepting whatever He had in store for me, His timetable, His will.

I would wait.

After all these years, Isaac still treasured me. I leaned into his embrace, thankful the Lord God had chosen me for this man and for His purpose. I hadn't thought to pray about my barrenness. I had not thought to pray at all but now…I would!

Soon my monthly cycle stopped and I was pregnant! I had not known such joy since the day I came to Isaac. I began to experience fluttering and slight movement in my stomach. I placed my hand there but the movement was gone. Another time, and yet another. My dream was confirmed.

It had happened! God had answered Isaac's prayer! I could think of nothing but the child I would birth. He would be an ideal man, just like his father and his grandfathers. I thanked God daily for the privilege He gave me. I spent hours thinking of names and imagining what color his hair and eyes would be. I had begun dreaming about the future again, knowing I would have a family of my own soon. Had other mothers felt this way? Sure they had not known this much joy, I was more grateful. My days were more joyful than I had known in a very long time.

The months passed and the baby grew inside my womb. Things were different now. There was a terrible commotion inside and I could find no comfort, not even for a moment. I struggled for relief but a battle was raging inside my womb. I was embarrassed to go to the other women. In all the years I sat with them to listen to their birthing stories, I never heard any woman mention this kind of trouble. They seemed so serene, confident. I knew so little about becoming a mother. I needed my mother. I was restless and very afraid. I could not tell Isaac for he would worry. He was so happy for me. But, if all was well, then why was I experiencing this? Desperate, I knew what I should do. What I must do.

I went to the Lord God just as I had seen Isaac do. I laid my concern before Him. "Why is this happening to me?"

I paused with my head bowed…not expecting what came next…God spoke!

I sat stunned and breathless as He spoke this prophecy. "Rebekah, Rebekah."

"Is that You LORD?"

"Yes, Rebekah, I am the God of Abraham, Isaac, and you also. This is what is happening and what will happen afterwards."

His words were like those of a friend. "The sons in your womb will become two nations. From the very beginning, the two nations will be rivals. One nation will be stronger than the other; and your older son will serve your younger son."

But, I was confused. One stronger…younger served by the older… how odd. This was against every tradition known to man. And, what did it all mean, giving birth to two sons at one time and from one conception? I had never heard of this. So strange, this message from God. I kept it all in my heart.

My time of delivery came, just as the Lord had said, "Two sons,"… that is the exactly the way it was. Twin babies. My firstborn was red as if he were sunburned at birth. His skin had thick hair like a furry coat. I knew his name, without question. It was breathed into my heart. "We will name him Esau"—hairy.

I remembered again God's prophecy….

As his brother was born, he griped Esau's heel. My second son, of whom the prophecy said would one day rule the elder, was born. And here, too, the name was there, on my lips. "My son's name is Jacob"—one who takes the heel.

And yet, the name held other meanings. Supplanter. Deceiver….

But one such as this would not be my son. My Jacob would be a man among men.

I relished in motherhood and at sixty years old, Isaac embraced being a father as if these two were direct gifts from God. They were. How he loved his sons!

As the boys grew, it was clear that Jacob possessed wisdom beyond his brother. He outwitted Esau in strategic games. I stepped outside one day to call the boys to eat. Jacob was wrestling Esau and I feared what might happen since Jacob was so wiry and quick. Much more than Esau.

At my call, Jacob released his hold to let Esau slip away.

"I'll get you next time."

Jacob smiled at his brother. "You know I always win."

On another day, I noticed Jacob setting up games that required agility. Esau could not possibly match his brother's skill, making him sure to lose. But Esau never gave up. His determination drove him to keep trying for a victory. One night, as Esau sat at his father's feet and listened to stories of Abraham and Ishmael hunting and bringing in their game. Isaac told Esau of his love for the taste of this wild game. Something changed and from that moment, he had nothing more to do with Jacob's games. Esau would become his father's man.

And so he did.

He became a skillful hunter, and his father delighted in eating his wild game. At last, he had found something in which he excelled.

Esau loved the great outdoors. His passion and lack of fear led him to take risks, live for the moment, and want things now. What he had not learned from his father was patience—but oh—he was a manly man. His very appearance commanded fear from his enemies. His stature combined with his hairy looks struck terror in all who opposed him. Still he was a rugged and handsome man. And yet, for all that and more, Isaac loved Esau best.

Unlike me, he was not aware of God's prophecy.

My Jacob, although a quiet man, possessed wisdom beyond his years. He approached every problem with strategy and determination. He relied upon God. I believed because of God's revelation to me, my job was to protect Jacob so he could one day fulfill His Promise.

I sighed. "My son, Jacob." I loved him best.

One day, Jacob cooked some lentil stew. I sat in another room separated from my son by a goat's-hair curtain but the tempting aroma of his stew made my mouth water. Just then, Esau arrived from the wilderness, exhausted and hungry. He had returned after three days empty-handed, something that seldom happened.

"I'm starving!" He thundered.

Such a harsh tone he used with his brother! Always demanding, never asking, this one.

"Give me some of that red pottage."

Jacob's reply was calm, soothing. Such wisdom my son had. "All right, I will give you some stew, but trade me your rights as firstborn son."

I held my breath. How did Jacob dare make such a request? Had he pondered it before? Surely, Esau would refuse. And yet, the Lord had promised. Would this be the way God intended? Would this be the day?

"Look, I'm dying of starvation!" Esau's tone was desperate now. "What good is my birthright to me if I am dead?"

"First you must swear that your birthright is mine!" Jacob spoke with such intention. He was shrewd.

I could not believe the words that followed for as quick as Jacob spoke, Esau swore the oath, thereby selling all his rights as the firstborn to his brother!

Only then did Jacob give his brother the bread and lentil stew.

Had Esau not considered that passing his birthright would forever establish Jacob as the patriarch of Isaac's family and on to the next generation? If he did, then he considered it to be of no more value than a bowl of lentil stew.

I sighed. Oh Esau. Do you not realize what have you done? Jacob now has all the inheritance and you have nothing.

Did he know the shift of power of this family had just changed? To give away his right of the firstborn…to become the spiritual leader of the family and the promise given to Abraham and Isaac, all this, would pass to Jacob.

I had seen the hand of God at work. This was His will. How else could it be done? I was in awe of the invisible God of Abraham.

If Isaac were to hear of this, how would he respond? He might die on hearing it!

Who would tell him?

Not I!

So, I kept silent….

The years passed, Isaac's eyes grew dim, and he called for his firstborn. It was time to bestow his blessing. And so, unaware of the agreement between his sons, Isaac called for Esau.

My firstborn stood by his father's bed.

I stood close, listening.

My husband's voice still held the authority of his years. "I am an old man now and I don't know when I may die. Take your bow and a quiver full of arrows, and go out into the open country to hunt some venison for me. Then make me savory food, such as I love, and bring it to me that I may eat, that my soul may bless you before I die."

"Yes, my father. I will do as you have said."

Realizing what was about to transpire, this blessing would give Esau power over his brother. I remembered again God's words of promise, "The older will serve the younger." If I did not act, God's promise would be thwarted.

Esau hurried to the woods to fulfill Isaac's request. And I? I paced the floor.

I hadn't expected this transference so soon. I had not worried since the day I overheard their exchange. Had not Esau told his father of this? His actions answered my question as I watched him bolt out of the tent.

I took a deep breath and exhaled with concern. I clenched my fist. I would *not* stand by to let this come to pass! Let Esau receive the blessing? No, never.

I loved my firstborn son, but he would make a terrible successor to

Isaac. Esau spent all his time roaming the woods for wild game to satisfy his own appetite and bringing in what Isaac loved. What was worse, though, was that he did not follow the ways of God. Had he not already married two pagan women who worshiped other gods? His wives drove both Isaac and me crazy. Their loud manner and constant chatter annoyed me to no end. Why couldn't he have chosen a good wife like me, or been content with just one wife, as was his father?

Jacob had strong faith. I often observed him worshipping at the altar of God as Isaac and Abraham did. Had not God promised, "The younger will rule the eldest?" So my path was clear. I must act to make sure God's promise was fulfilled before it was too late.

Why else then, would God reveal such truth to me? I could—and should—change the course of Isaac's intentions.

I was the only one who could.

I went to my favored son. "Jacob, listen, I overheard your father tell Esau to bring him some wild game and prepare him a delicious meal, for then he will bless him in the presence of the Lord."

Jacob did not speak. My wise son waited to hear all I had to say.

"Now, my son, listen to me. Do as I tell you! Go out to the flocks, and bring me two fine young goats. I'll prepare your father's favorite dish. Then you can be the one to take the stew to your father. He will eat it and bless you instead, before he dies."

Jacob shook his head, holding out his arms. "But look! Esau is a hairy man, and my skin is smooth. What if my father touches me? He'll see that I'm trying to trick him, and then he'll curse me instead of blessing me."

I grasped Jacob's arm. "Then let the curse fall on me, my son! Do as I have told you. Go out and get the goats!"

I prepared the delicious meal, just the way Isaac liked it. Using fresh herbs and spices, I disguised the goat meat to taste like venison stew. But my son's words plagued me—until I had an idea! I took the skins of a goat and bound them on Jacobs's arms and neck. I brought Esau's clothes for him. Now Jacob would smell and feel like his brother!

Finally, I gave Jacob the meal, including fresh, warm bread. He questioned me no more. He took what I handed him and went to the bed of his father.

I listened just outside the room.

"My father?"

"Yes, my son, who are you—Esau or Jacob?"

"It's Esau, your firstborn son. I've done as you told me. Here is the wild game. Now sit up in your bed and prepare to eat so you can give me your blessing."

"How did you find it so quickly, my son?"

My heart chilled within me. How would my Jacob answer his father?

"The Lord your God put it before me!"

Such a wise one, my son!

"Come closer so I can touch you and make sure that you are indeed Esau."

I heard Jacob move closer to his father, could envision Isaac touching him.

"The voice is Jacob's, but the hands are Esau's."

For all the uncertainty in my husband's voice, he did not recognize Jacob. So Isaac prepared to offer the blessing. I waited, holding my breath, for the words to come. But when Isaac spoke again, it was not the blessing.

"Are you really my son Esau?" Something had not set right with his father.

Oh dear, could Jacob continue this deception?

"I am!"

My son's answer came without hesitation. So firm was he, that Isaac was convinced.

Jacob was in firstborn position with all the rights thereof since his trade with Esau. And now the spiritual mantle of his father would be transferred to him as well.

"Now, my son, bring me the wild game. Let me eat it, and then I will give you my blessing."

I pressed a hand over my heart as I heard Isaac eating, the wine being poured. My heart pounded. Would the blessing never come?

Then, at last, Isaac spoke again. "Please come a little closer and kiss me, my son."

I could not help it…I peered through the goat's hair curtain to watch as Jacob bowed down and kissed his father. My eyes widened when Isaac took hold of the clothes Jacob wore and smelled them! Oh, how clever my husband.

But I was clever too. The clothes on Jacob's back were Esau's.

"Ah! Surely, the smell of my son is like the smell of the field, which the Lord has blessed! Therefore,"

I waited breathless, could not rest until he was through. Go on Isaac….

"May God give you of the dew of heaven, of the fatness of the earth, and plenty of grain and wine. Let peoples serve you, and nations bow down to you. Be master of your brethren, and let your mother's sons bow down to you. Cursed be everyone who curses you, and blessed be those who bless you!"

I leaned back against the tent wall.

It was done.

When Esau returned from his hunt, I stood in the shadows and watched him prepare a delicious stew. He brought it to his father.

I followed my son Esau, careful he didn't see me.

He entered Isaac's room. His booming voice rang out. "Sit up, my father, and eat my wild game so you can give me your blessing."

"Who are you?"

The confusion in Isaac's voice tore at my heart. Once again, I leaned in to peer past the curtain. How would my husband react?

How would Esau?

"It's your son, your firstborn son Esau."

Isaac's voice and hands trembled. "Then who just served me wild game? I have already eaten it and blessed him just before you came. And, bless him indeed I did and this cannot be changed. The blessing must stand!"

At his father's words, Esau cried out. Never had I heard such raw agony, such a sound of—betrayal.

Supplanter…Deceiver….

I closed my eyes against the accusations.

"Oh, my father, what about me? Bless me, too!"

"I cannot. Your brother came with deceit and has taken away your blessing."

Such sorrow in my husband's voice—and such rage in Esau's!

"Is he not rightly named Jacob, for he has cheated me twice? First, he took my rights as the firstborn, and now he has stolen my blessing. Please, Father, haven't you saved even one blessing for me?"

"I have made Jacob your master and declared all his brothers will be his servants. I guaranteed him an abundance of grain and wine—I have given it all to him. What is left for me to give you, my son? There is no more."

Isaac was right. The blessing of a father was irrevocable. Invoked on earth and sustained in Heaven.

"But have you just one blessing? Oh my father, bless me, too!" My firstborn was sobbing now, great rending sounds as though his very heart was being torn from his body.

Supplanter…Deceiver….

I barely withheld a groan. For now, our son Esau had realized the full weight of the two things he had lost. He was suffering. He had just faced the most serious moment of his life. The reality of selling his birthright, and now losing his blessing was almost more than he could bear.

Had not I served God by my actions? Why, then, this great sorrow wrenching my heart? There was but one answer. In helping one son…

I had betrayed the other.

I preferred one, loved them both, but in this hour my actions were necessary to fulfill the prophecy spoken by God. The older shall serve the younger….

What was done was done. Esau's woeful sobs poured down like driving rain on the roof. I longed to go in, comfort him, but I dared not.

They must never know I saw or heard.

Bode before his father—Isaac placed his hands on Esau's head. He took a long, hard breath. "You'll live far from earth's bounty, remote from Heaven's dew. You'll live by your sword, hand-to-mouth, and you'll serve your brother. But when you can't take it anymore, you'll break loose and run free."

My blood chilled, for Esau's blessing...

Was a curse.

Everything had changed.

From the moment of his brother's betrayal, the anger of Esau could not be requited. He walked as a man bent on destruction. Not his own.

I heard commotion in Esau's tent, such ramblings, and noise coming from within. I stepped closer. I heard his voice bellowing. "I will soon be mourning my father's death. I will kill my brother, Jacob, giving me all the rights, and as an only son I will receive all the inheritance."

I was determined to protect Jacob. With the state that Esau was in, he would not wait. If he met his brother face to face, Jacob would die.

I hurried to him. "Esau is consoling himself by plotting to kill you. Listen carefully, my son. Get ready to flee to the house of my brother, Laban, in Haran. Stay with him until your brother no longer seeks to harm you. When he forgets what you have done to him, I will send for you. Why should I lose you both at once?"

Oh, I hadn't expected this uprising! The curse I said would fall on me now ravaged Jacob. But, I would be judged for my behavior. Now I would live without my beloved son, for I knew not how long. This was far from my dreams for us all. Now he must run for his life. He must flee—or die.

Within the power of his words, Isaac had established what would happen upon his death. All the wealth amassed by Abraham and Isaac and promises made to them by God would pass on to Jacob, and then to his children and their children. And, without me, it would not have happened this way. Now I must be sure everything went according to my plan...God's plan.

But, I needed Isaac to be the one to send Jacob away. I had yet another plan.

I would go to Isaac.

What had happened in this place today, and the chain of events it would foster, would set destinies into motion. Something that could not change, even for eternity.

Isaac heard me enter and looked in my direction. "Rebekah, is that you?"

"Yes Isaac, I need your wisdom. We have difficulty here in our home. You know the grief Esau's Canaanite wives have caused us. Now I must ask you. What are we going to do to insure this doesn't happen to Jacob? I would rather die than see him marry a Canaanite!"

Isaac thought for only a moment. "He should not marry one of those pagan women. You are right. They have caused much trouble in our home. Please send Jacob to me that I may give him instruction."

So Isaac told him, "You must not marry any of these Canaanite women. Instead, go at once to Haran, to the house of your grandfather Bethuel, and marry one of your uncle Laban's daughters. They are part of the covenant line of blessing the Lord God has made to us."

Jacob nodded. He understood what his father said. He would go at once but not before Isaac spoke more, repeating the blessing.

"May God Almighty bless you and give you many children. And may your descendants multiply and become many nations! May God pass on to you and your descendants the blessings he promised to my father Abraham. May you own this land where you are now living as a foreigner, for God promised this land to Abraham and his descendants."

Now it was Isaac sending Jacob away. My plan had worked. Jacob's destiny lay before him and through my actions, he was now in God's hands.

Ready to leave me.

By sending Jacob to my family. He would be out of harm's way. But, a mother worries, would he be safe there? For he was no longer safe in the shelter of my home. But in Haran….

Jacob would travel the same route I had taken here. I came to fulfill my dream, and had fulfilled a promise Eliezer made to Abraham. I had come to possess my inheritance, and Jacob was walking away from his.

I watched for a long time, as his figure grew smaller in the distance and I could no longer see him. He was walking away from me…out of my sight, and out of my life.

Jacob was gone from my presence, Isaac gone from my confidence, and Esau and those abrasive Hittite wives…gone! He went toward the Dead Sea to join his uncle Ishmael, Isaacs's brother, and there he took a third wife. Isaac said Ishmael and Esau had a common thread…they were both denied their birthright. Now I prayed God would one day enable my firstborn to forgive his brother.

And his mother.

Isaac and I were childless again. Just as we had been in the twenty years before we had the twins. I was not at peace then and I was not at peace now. The house was quiet, too quiet, thanks to the absence of Esau's wives. If Isaac knew I had orchestrated the great deception, he never mentioned it.

My what if's began. What if I had prayed first…waited on God? My actions brought consequences, more grief, more sorrow, and more strife. My judgment caught me in a hailstorm without protection. I had not the comfort of Isaac. I stepped around his intention, and out his covering, God's covering. I stood alone, knee deep and helpless in the storm of my life. What would happen to us now? In getting what I thought God wanted, my soul was in a state of distress.

Until…

I could stand it no longer. I went to my husband one day with passion on my lips and purpose in my heart. I had sheltered these things long enough. It was time to tell Isaac.

Early that morning, I went to his chamber. "Isaac?"

"Yes, my beloved."

"May I sit with you awhile? I have things I must share."

"Of course Rebekah, I sense your heart is heavy, but first come, and let me feel the warmth of your embrace."

"Oh Isaac, if you don't despise me after hearing what I need to tell you, then, and only then will I feel worthy of your embrace."

"Then tell me at once, Rebekah."

I sighed. Where to begin. At the beginning. "When I was pregnant, before I knew we had twins, there was turmoil in my womb. I was frightened and quiet embarrassed to ask the other women. I went to God for help. In my prayer, I asked. 'Why is this happening to me?'"

"Isaac, you might not believe this but God spoke to me! And, when He did, I was startled, so much that I trembled. Here is what He said. 'The sons in your womb will become two nations. From the very beginning, the two nations will be rivals. One nation will be stronger than the other; and your older son will serve your younger son.'"

"Rebekah, why did you not tell me these things?"

"I don't know. I was shocked that He said I had two sons in my womb. I had never heard of twins. I was terrified. I should have come to you at that time but I waited to see if indeed two lived inside me. Then I was so thrilled at your joy of their birth, I put it aside without giving it more thought. I diminished its truth, even doubting what I heard. It seemed so unbelievable."

"You forgot?"

"When I overheard Esau trade his birthright to Jacob for a meal, the prophecy God gave me stormed into my mind again and I told myself, "It is happening, it is beginning! Just as God said."

I looked full into Isaac's face.

"As I pondered choosing the moment to reveal all these things to you, I heard you tell Esau you were going to bestow your blessing upon him. And, because of the prophecy given to me, I could not let that happen. And so, I devised a plan to thwart your intention. Today I am here on bended knee, to beg your forgiveness."

Bowing, I rested my head on his lap. He placed those still strong hands upon my gray head.

Tears flowed through my words. "Will you forgive me…for not honoring you by telling you these things…for acting without your authority, and for deceiving you?"

I lifted my head. Waited for his response.

He cradled my face in his hands. "It all makes sense to me now! All this has been the hand of God. I am glad you were the vessel that brought about all these events."

Now it was his turn to weep.

Still, I had to know. "But do you forgive me?"

"Of course you are forgiven, of course I love you, and of course God spoke the truth to you. I wish you had come sooner. I am sorry your soul was troubled over these things."

He told me that the will of God prevails in spite of the actions of his people. His words calmed me, restoring his trust I thought I had forever lost.

"Rebekah, although we make mistakes, God does not."

Isaac's faith and his humble way of waiting on the Lord God brought me more comfort and renewed faith. I would trust Him more for the days I had left.

What if…I had shared God's prophecy with Isaac sooner, how would it have changed things? Isaac would have loved Jacob as I did, treated him as firstborn. Through his wisdom, all the needs of Esau would have been met. There would have been peace and harmony in our home. I would be resting in the shadow of his covering.

Instead, there remains this separation, jealously, and hatred. What a price for not waiting on God. I lived with heartache for I was a mother without her children. Two sons gone, no grandchildren to hold, and a rift in my family that only God could heal. My joy of mothering departed yes, but I still had sweet and precious times with Isaac.

I lived to see Esau overcome his great loss to be the progenitor of a great tribe in Edom. Jacob remained far away in Haran but when he returns someday, he will receive his inheritance. From Abraham, to Isaac, and to Jacob…

But these things I will not see. Nor will I hold Jacob's children in my arms or kiss them goodnight.

For now, I know that I am dying….

All those years in between our children leaving and my illness overtaking me, I cared for Isaac. In his haste to bless his sons, we both thought his death was near, leaving me to die alone. And now, I will pass, leaving him to bury me. He will be the one to welcome Jacob…when he returns to claim his inheritance.

The years with Isaac and my boys have passed like a mist coming in from the sea. Though I lost much, in trying to make life happen, showing favorites, and wanting more, I am now at peace. I understand and am grateful knowing I have a little time to be at rest with my life, to be at peace with my future, and be content with my passing.

I lie on my bed, waiting, waiting.

My breathing is shallow, but my mourning turns to joy as I revisit my life journey. I never dreamed my passing would bring me this much peace.

The nurses attend me but it is Isaac's tender touch and the comfort of his forgiveness that soothes me.

I know without a doubt, the loving arms of God, my father, await me.

That is enough.

Read Rebekah's story in Genesis 24-27

Chapter 5
Leah

IN THE DARKNESS of the wedding tent, I lay. Breathless….

I had taken my sister's place.

And I had stolen her most treasured possession. One she had waited seven years to receive.

Her husband.

On her wedding night.

Tears rolled off my face and pooled onto my gown, but the man beside me would not know. Not yet. Had not father made sure?

He whispered her name even as he slept. "Rachel, Rachel…"

I did not, could not, correct him. He would know soon enough.

There was no undoing the deed already done.

I was Jacob's wife.

And my beautiful sister Rachel was left…still waiting.

Jacob loved Rachel the moment he met her—loved everything about her, the look of her, and the very idea of her. From the beginning, they possessed a God-given connection. I saw it. Our family saw it. It was evident every time he gazed into her dazzling eyes, that he adored her more every day. Soon everyone knew his passion, for he was in love with my younger sister, Rachel.

Their union was to be another great love story of our family's history, rivaling that of Rebekah at the well. Until father…

He changed everything.

Jacob was our cousin. In fact, our Aunt Rebekah's son, who came to Haran from the faraway land of Canaan. He sought refuge. And a wife. He got both. He just didn't know that to get the wife he wanted, he must take two.

My sister, Rachel, was a striking beauty. She smiled, exposing flawless white teeth, and dimples adorned her face. She embodied such charisma and sparkle. The truth is, she added color to my world. We were so close. I loved being with her because everything looked promising through Rachel's eyes. I was content to live in her shadow.

But I relished the fact that as the oldest daughter, I would marry first.

I was ready and waiting for these arrangements to be completed. It was a father's obligation to see that this tradition was honored. Such unions were prearranged during early lives, perhaps even as infants by family patriarchs. But not for me, not yet. When the time was right, father would make proper plans. I was sure of it. These weddings guaranteed a father's wealth passed properly and that covenant bloodlines would not be broken. Love was not a consideration he had said, but might develop, so I waited. And I dreamed.

Rachel was happiest outside. She loved everything about the outdoors: The sun, fresh air, the sky, the trees, the wildflowers, and most of all, she loved our sheep. Even as a toddler, she had gone with Father to the pasture. Through the years, she claimed the sheep as her own and tended them as so. Father always said. "Our Rachel is a dreamer, just like her Aunt Rebekah. She is most happy running, chasing, carrying, and naming the lambs."

And I was most like mother. I loved everything about the spaces inside our home. I took to mothering my younger brothers naturally, and minding them made me long for children of my own. I would be a great mother. I enjoyed cooking, sewing, keeping the house, and preserving food. From the earliest age, I made breads, stews, cakes, and roasted meats.

Mother taught me well, telling me often, "Leah, you are a good homemaker. You will make a great wife for a fortunate man someday."

Someday. I was ready for my someday.

When Jacob came, he added adventure to our lives. He worked long, hard hours for one month and then asked my father's permission to marry Rachel. He promised to work for seven years as his dowry. "I have left my inheritance with my father in Canaan. If you will accept my offer, I will return there with Rachel, but only when my debt to you is paid."

Seven years. Such a dowry for love. I wanted the kind of love this dowry described.

"Very well." Father smiled, and I could tell he was more than pleased.

Jacob had proven he was a gifted and industrious young man, which only made life easier for Father. As time went on, Jacob's work brought him a finer quality of livestock. He was brilliant in these matters and his watchful eye allowed the herds to grow without loss from disease or other dangers. The livestock increased each year. Jacob's hard work and God-given talent were making Father a wealthy man.

But all Jacob lived and breathed for was Rachel. It was hard not to be jealous of his adoration. How I longed to step into her shoes, even for a day, experiencing what such devotion would evoke.

The years passed with no marriage arrangement for me. I knew of no available men in our village. My hope dwindled with each passing day. Tradition would be skipped and Rachel would marry before me. Hot tears sprang without my permission to honor my grief. Father said nothing.

I cannot say when his deception began or how long he had planned it. Perhaps it was from the very beginning, or after he saw what a great worker Jacob was, or when he realized how much personal benefit he would gain. But at some point, he had developed a plan. His plan.

All this time, Jacob had become a loved and treasured part of our family. He fit in so beautifully. Our lives were enriched by his presence. Especially mine. The sad reality for me was that he soon he would leave us and take Rachel with him to his homeland. The years had passed too quickly, but Jacob numbered each day as a day closer to realizing his dream. Rachel said he etched a mark on the big myrtle tree for every month that passed.

Even though I was on the outside of their dream, somehow its beauty captivated me.

Finally, the covenant time passed and Jacob approached my father. Mother, Rachel, and I listened behind the curtain.

"Laban, I have completed the contract. I gave you seven years of labor for Rachel. It is time to give her to me so I can marry her."

Father spoke at last. "Very well, Jacob, I will begin the wedding preparations."

We all breathed a sigh of relief. Father was not always forthcoming in honoring his commitments. Mother clapped her hands as we stepped into the room. How she loved weddings! Now it was her turn to put one on. "Leah and I will make it beautiful, just like a dream. You have been patient, Jacob, waiting so long for this day."

Jacob shook his head. "But no! All these years, they seemed but as a day, because of my love for Rachel."

Because of my love, because of my love….

His words took my breath. I would never forget them. They were poetry to my ears.

And to Rachel. Her lips curled into a happy smile. She could barely contain her enchantment.

So father had passed over the tradition upon which I had built all my hopes and dreams. It was now a reality.

I could almost hear everyone's sentiments.

Poor Leah.

And so I would be known for the rest of my life because we had run out of time for me.

Our home came alive with wedding plans. We made lists and sent messages to friends and family in the villages nearby. Mother and I spread the news at the marketplace and at the well.

Rachel lived in her dream world while mother and I preserved and put away food. Father busied himself by gathering enough wine for a year! Mother sewed my sister's magnificent wedding dress, but Rachel wanted to design her own bridal veil. I watched my sister stitch and re-stitch until it was perfect for her. She tried it on every day imagining *the* day as she twirled around, pretending Jacob was dancing with her across the room. I was happy for her.

But still….

Out-of-town guests arrived and pitched tents on our property in preparation for the celebration, which would happen the next day.

That night Rachel and I sat up until the early hours of the morning, reliving our years together and sharing what might be in her future. My sister would be a married woman tomorrow. We giggled about the rituals that would take place at the wedding and those afterward. After such imagining, it was hard for either of us to sleep.

Morning came, bringing with it Rachel's wedding day.

Mother and I attended Rachel. First, we brought her breakfast and ate with her. We recited the schedule and assured her everything was perfect. She need not worry about anything today.

She bathed and we helped wash her long, dark tresses and sat in the sun while her hair dried. We brushed and pinned the locks high atop her head. She was radiant. Mother put her own pearls at Rachel's neck. At last, she stepped into her beautiful dress and slipped into her sandals. The bride was ready. But, I wished it were me, instead.

It was a beautiful day in Haran. The weather could not have been better, perfect for a wedding in every way. The servants brought out the banquet food, such a magnificent feast set for all. My eyes beheld all the elements that had gone into making this special day for my sister. I was proud. It was just right for Rachel.

As the party began, I looked down the tables to see many dishes of lamb, meat kabobs, roasted tomatoes, eggplant, Jerusalem artichokes, onions, bell peppers, and Lebanese grape leaf rolls. I took a plate. My favorites were curry cabbage rolls and Burma bread. I filled a plate for Rachel, knowing she would not eat much, but she loved the olives and flatbread.

Music floated in the air. Guests danced between courses of food. So much wine consumed! But Rachel and I would not partake for we wanted to remember every detail and every moment. The servants continued to pour for the guests. Many had more than their share, Jacob included. Father seemed intent on keeping his son- in- law's cup full.

"No cup to remain empty tonight!"

In the midst of the festivities, Father stood to speak. His voice was loud and steady. He spread his arms open in a sweeping gesture. "Thank you all for coming to the marriage celebration of my daughter to Jacob, from Canaan. Please continue enjoying the celebration, there is much food and wine for all. And, don't forget to have something from the sweet table: walnut and date cakes, baklava, and other tasty treats."

But, wait….father had forgotten to mention one thing.

Rachel's name! How odd.

Jacob walked among the guests, who told stories of Rachel as a child. She was a happy, blushing bride. All eyes were on her, adoring her, happy for her.

Soon Father would take, or rather guide, Jacob to his place in the wedding tent, which he had prepared. Then he would escort Rachel, veiled, into the wedding tent.

When it was time, I walked inside the house with Rachel. She took off her veil and went to her room. I kissed her good night, went to my room, and dressed for bed. I laid down, reliving the moments of the joyous day, a beautiful love story from beginning to en—

Someone jerked back the curtain to my room. I sat up. "Father!"

"Be very quiet and come with me!"

"Why…what is it?" I rose and followed as he commanded.

He led me the short distance between our house and the wedding tent. "What I am about to tell you is for your ears only."

My heart raced. "But Father, what are you doing?"

"Leah, you must obey me. For what I am about to do, I take full responsibility. You will go into the wedding tent and become Jacob's wife tonight."

"No, Father, please I cannot! Can I? What will Rachel…

"Be still! Obey me and do exactly as I say."

"Why, Father?"

"It is for the best, you will see. I must first take care of you, my daughter. Am I not bound by this tradition? You are the one who will become Jacob's first wife tonight. Then, after a time, Rachel can fulfill her dream and become a wife to Jacob."

I looked down to see Rachel's veil in his hand.

I was trapped—torn between the joys of being the wife to a man I adored and betraying my sister. I couldn't help myself.

I chose Jacob.

As we neared the wedding tent, I paused. "What if he recognizes me and asks me to leave?"

"Daughter, it is not possible in his drunken state for him to recognize you. Of this, I have made sure."

He placed Rachel's veil on me, pulled back the door to the tent and…I walked in.

It was dark except for the faint glow of one small candle, which allowed me to see Jacob lying on the bed. I spoke not a word. I could not speak, lest he discover the truth. With bitter sweetness and awareness that this was now my wedding night, I put out the candle, slipped into the bed and into his embrace.

The deception had worked. He had mistaken me for his beloved. He was now my husband.

As he drifted into slumber, He uttered her name. "Rachel, Rachel." He reached to stroke my hair. I let him, but I was not who he thought. I was not his beloved. But I was his wife.

Jacob was fast asleep. I was not.

I had what I wanted. Rachel would have to wait.

I hoped she would see this was Father's doing and forgive me, someday. I would never let her know how willing I had been.

But though she would be upset, even angry, I was Jacob's wife, and nothing but death could change the fact.

I gazed at the sleeping, contented figure at my side. How could my fulfilled dream now bring guilt?

How had our father kept Rachel away all night?

I would know soon enough.

As the early morning light flooded through the seams in the tent, I stared at Jacob's face. He stirred. He opened his eyes and looked at me—

And recoiled. He sat up—rubbing his eyes, then looked at me again. As understanding dawned, he cried out. "No!"

He put on his tunic and raced from the tent.

I heard shouting. No, screaming.

I peered out from the tent. Jacob was shaking, his fists were clenched, and his face was crimson. I saw the veins in his neck. Was he going to attack Father?

"Laban, you deceiver! How could you be so wicked? How could you do this to Rachel?"

"Jacob, my son." With a wave of his hand, Father dismissed my husband's anger and made light of those he had hurt by his actions. "It's not our custom here to marry off a younger daughter ahead of the older. I am bound by tradition and in time, both you and Rachel will come to understand why I had to do this."

Jacob's voice boomed out in the morning air. "But I do not love Leah! My heart belongs *only* to Rachel."

Jacob's grief-filled words pierced my heart. Hadn't I known this? But my love for him convinced me go ahead with Father's plan. I looked back to see father, still composed. He spoke in a low, mild tone, very much in contrast to Jacob's bellows. "My son, wait until Leah's bridal week is over, then I'll give you Rachel too—provided you promise to work another seven years for me."

Jacob raged even more. "Laban, at your hand, I have been deceived twice!" He paused as if making sure each word was exactly as he wished. "You are not a man of honor, and, you are not as shrewd as you think."

His next words took everyone by surprise. "The love I have for Rachel is far beyond what you could ever understand. I will give you seven more years of my life, but had you realized the depth of my love, you could have had me as your servant forever!"

After he had proclaimed his powerful truths, Jacob's appearance changed. It was as though clarity had come to him. The weight of his injustice broke free as he spoke. "Let it be known to you this day, Oh Laban, My God will judge you for this deception, as he has judged me for mine."

Jacob was quiet now. He looked back to the tent, saw that I had heard his words, and acknowledged me.

It was enough.

The wedding tent…the wedding week. One I would never forget. I wanted Jacob to remember my embrace…his time with me, my kisses. When he left this tent, he would know that this wife loved him also. I would not regret or waste one moment.

I prepared to go to my father's house alone when my week passed. I opened the door to see Father, bringing Rachel to the wedding tent. I looked down at her veil in my hands and for the first time asked myself. "Why did I do it?

I dismissed the thought—I knew why.

Jacob's joy was complete now that he and Rachel were one. But it was not so with Rachel. She would forever deal with the truth that I was also Jacob's wife. And that I had stolen him from her.

The truth was we all lost Rachel the night of her great sadness. She was not the person she had been. I feared she would never get over my father betraying her, me for my part, or Jacob for letting it happen. My expressions of love to her were unanswered, as were my efforts to gain acceptance from Jacob, though I would never give up needing their love. Buried in my heart was the resolve that I would and could make Jacob love me.

I was wrong.

I cried out to Jacob's God as I had seen him do many times in his worship. "Please make Jacob love me." The Lord saw I was unloved and gave me the gift of children instead.

Rachel had Jacob, but I? I had his baby. Perhaps he would love me now for giving him an heir. I may not be able to hold Jacob as often as I wanted but I would have our child to hold.

I wore my pregnancy like a crown. A part of Jacob grew inside me. I gave birth to a son, and named him Reuben.

I was first to the wedding tent and first to the birthing tent, but not… the first loved.

I conceived again. The Lord God was once again showing me favor. Another son. Simeon. No child for Rachel. To my surprise, I bore a third son, Levi. I flaunted my ability to conceive, like a flag of victory over the house of Jacob. Again, pregnant and giving birth to another son, Judah.

Was God making up for the love I missed?

With four fine sons born to Jacob, I stopped having children.

But Rachel… still could not conceive. She ached for a child so much that she took an extreme measure. She gave her handmaiden Bilhah to Jacob as a wife. She told him, "Bilhah will bear children for me and through her I can be a mother too." For Rachel to share her husband with yet another woman proved how desperate she had become.

Bilhah conceived and had Jacob's fifth son. Rachel named him Dan. Bilhah became pregnant again and gave Jacob his sixth son. Rachel named him Naphtali. She acted as though she had born these sons. She communicated her delight before the entire camp saying, "I have struggled hard with my sister, and I'm winning!"

Oh Rachel, not…even…close!

Something burned within me. I would not be outdone. I took my servant, Zilpah, and gave her to Jacob as a wife. Rachel had not thought of the complications of three wives for Jacob, so now she could deal with four as soon Zilpah bore son number seven. I named him Gad. Zilpah gave Jacob another child: son number eight. I named him Asher.

I was winning.

To my delight, God opened my womb again and I gave birth to Jacob's ninth son. I named him Issachar. I could hardly believe my good fortune because I conceived yet another time and gave a tenth son to Jacob, Zebulun.

What more could I ask? Could not Jacob see that God favored me? Would he not also favor me? But it was not to be, the love he had for Rachel would never be diminished. She was number one in his eyes and in every way. I could not change this, even if I bore him one hundred sons!

As if a special gift from God, for me. I bore one more child. A precious little girl I named Dinah. My first and only daughter.

Although my sister had two sons by her handmaiden, it was not enough. What she thought would bring her joy had faded. She had no child from her womb. The beautiful, lovely, and enchanted Rachel was barren. She would not know the joy of motherhood as I had.

My quiver was full, my heart content, but I could not make Jacob love me. Somewhere along the way, I came to peace with this reality and stopped trying so hard.

Then Jacob's God remembered Rachel's plight, answered her prayers, and opened her womb. She became pregnant. Her world came alive. Her color returned and the radiance and charisma of her youth came back. Her eyes sparkled and she was so happy. "God has removed my disgrace."

Rachel disgraced? She had Jacob! How could she be disgraced? A pang seized my heart. I realized that even his love was not enough to fulfill her dreams. She was shamed. Oh, that I had recognized this sooner! I had contributed to her pain. A great sorrow overcame me. It was then my love for her, suppressed somewhere within—broke forth into the light.

I was so sorry. I knew what I must do.

I went to Jacob's altar. The presence of God was there. I humbled my heart before Him. I surrendered my hostility and pride as I fell over the bench. My fingers touched the earth. I called out to God, begging His forgiveness. "What damage have I done in all the years by shutting my sister out of my love and my life? I have sinned. Please bring healing to Rachel and to me. Only You can mend our broken hearts."

I waited. Deep in my worship, I felt His tender, healing touch.

And then I felt a human touch on my shoulder. It was Rachel. With tears in her eyes, she faced me.

"I heard you Leah, as you prayed to God, I realized how much I love you and that I also am guilty. I was angry and jealous. Angry because you took my place, jealous because of God's blessing you with many children. The bitterness and unforgiveness was a barrier that prevented my heart from receiving or giving love, both to you and Jacob. Will you forgive me?"

"Oh Rachel, me forgive you? No, no my dear and precious sister, it is I who begs your pardon. In my greed and unrequited need for love, I flaunted my ability to bear children. I cannot make up for this injustice but if you forgive me, I will prove worthy of a loving sister. The burden of our separation will be mended, making us whole and complete again."

From our knees, we turned to sit on the altar. We embraced and cried on each other's shoulder. We celebrated as the love within us came forth. Oh, how we needed each other!

I know not how long we lingered but the sun had cast a shadow upon the altar. Our future and our families waited. I stood first to help Rachel from her perch. I placed my hand on her stomach that was full with new life. "God bless us all."

Jacob stood outside the entrance to the garden. A broad smile stretched across his face. He knew. Hand in hand, we walked toward him. He stretched wide his arms around the two of us…and we walked back united, as one family.

Weeks passed. We talked, shared, and laughed together—such a blessed time of healing. We ate together, made time for walks, and relived our childhood. We enjoyed all things sisters should. God was making up the years the locust had eaten away, leaving peace and harmony to rest on the house of Jacob.

At the first sign of Rachel's labor, I was there. She gave birth with ease to a son she named Joseph, and she said, "May the Lord add yet another son to my family." The pride and glow of motherhood radiated, making her more beautiful than ever.

Jacob raised the babe above his head dedicating him to God, who had lifted his beloved's burden and united his family.

For all these events and the joy that was in his heart, Jacob took a lamb from his herd, went to the altar, and made a sacrifice of thanksgiving to God. Jacob now had eleven sons, one daughter, and four wives.

It had been twenty-plus years since Jacob came to Haran. One day he called Rachel and me to the garden. He had something important to tell us.

"The Lord God spoke to me as He did to Abraham. He told me it was time to leave Haran. I am to go back to the Land of Canaan where I belong…to my brother, mother, and father. But I have a problem. I have worked for your father all these years yet he refuses to release me."

Father had never rewarded him with honest wages but Jacob's fortunes, because of God's blessing, had now exceeded the wealth of our father. Even though he had taken advantage of Jacob from the beginning, God had blessed his herds. Father's greed had damaged everyone. Jacob had our full support. We were more than anxious to leave. An air of happiness swept over me.

"We will go when your father is away shearing his sheep. You must pack everything and be ready to leave at the moment I tell you." With Jacob's instruction, it was settled.

I looked out my door to Rachel's home. She would be packing up her household, as was I. Jacob had given the signal. Father was departing on his trip and the very minute he was out of sight, we would leave, taking all our servants, household goods, and the livestock we had acquired though Jacob's hard work and God's grace.

I saw Rachel going toward Father's home with an empty pack. Soon she returned with the pack bulging. I motioned for her to come at once for everyone had gathered for our departure.

Our large caravan moved slowly, leaving Haran and all our turmoil and grief. We stopped at the well and filled our water vessels. This well had brought Jacob into our life. I was thankful.

I was glad to see the city of Haran disappear behind us. I was re-born and free, Jacob was free of bondage to Father, Rebekah and I were united, and our children were healthy. We were a family unit.

"Thank You, God!"

Our father caught up with us a week into our journey. Now he was the one who raged, for he had been deceived. God was indeed bringing judgment on Father as Jacob had pronounced that day outside our wedding tent. His fury exploded.

"Leaving without notice, Jacob, taking my daughters away, taking my grandchildren without allowing me to say good-bye, and why did you steal my gods?"

Jacob laughed. "Me, steal your worthless gods? Laban, you know I have never worshipped them!"

"Had it not been for your God warning me in a dream last night, not to touch or harm you, I would have forced you to return to Haran. I have brought with me enough men to make this happen if I so desire."

Jacob was not afraid. "Laban, please search our camp and if anyone had taken your idols, then they will not live!"

Father searched our entire camp but did not find the gods or anything else belonging to him. At last, he kissed us and left, dejected and humiliated by Jacob's words.

Haran had forever been a city of many idols. People bowed before their own created gods, ones they could see. But not Jacob, for he worshipped before The Invisible God. The Only True God of Heaven and earth.

How Father must have feared and trembled when God spoke directly to him, calling him by name, warning him not to touch Jacob. Never had his gods spoken. With God's warning terrifying his very being, he would not dare stand against Him. This was absolute confirmation that the God of Heaven reigned on earth and watched over His own. The family of Jacob would serve this Living, Eternal God.

We journeyed nearly five-hundred miles from Haran. Somewhere along the way, God spoke to Jacob and told him to get rid of all the idols in our camp. The servants had brought their deities, for they had known no other way.

Jacob called everyone together. "Surrender these idols as a dedication offering to the Lord God of Israel."

And all the people obeyed. None held back.

Jacob would bury them….we would cleanse ourselves, and change garments. Then, we would go to Bethel to repent and dedicate ourselves to God. There Jacob vowed his household would serve and worship no other gods. To Jacob, Bethel was God's Holy Ground, a special place where God first spoke to him on his flight from Esau to Haran.

It was then we discovered that Rachel had stolen Father's idols! I remembered Jacob's oath before my father: "If anyone here has taken your idols, they will not live!"

I was heartsick. I prayed for mercy. I looked at my sister but I didn't see panic in her features. Perhaps she took the idols to spite father. Did she bow to them or had she wanted to deny Father's worship? She trusted and believed in the Almighty God of Jacob. I recalled seeing her at the altar, heard her cry out to God for a baby. She had believed —and received a child.

I never spoke of it and I would never know her reasons.

Now that Jacob had dedicated his household to God, he waited for God to speak. Then, we would move to Hebron, where his inheritance waited with his mother and father. But first, he said. "Everything depends on my ability to make peace with my estranged twin brother Esau."

The rift between them must have to do with deception since his words to Father about God judging them both. Jacob prayed and then sent a message ahead to his brother's camp in the Negev to tell him of his coming.

Rachel approached me one night after our meal. "Walk with me?"

"Yes, my sister."

"Leah," she paused, fanning her hands, bringing fresh air to her face. She was excited to tell me her news.

"What Rachel? Please tell me! I cannot wait."

Her eyes were bigger than I had ever seen them. She beamed like the full moon on a cloudless night. "I am pregnant again!"

I hugged her. I held her hands as we jumped up and down. "I am so happy for you!"

I meant it.

Rachel rejoiced. The entire camp joined her. She was thrilled carrying another child for Jacob. I braided her hair while little Joseph played by her side. I massaged her back and rubbed her feet with fragrant oil. I was excited for the arrival of her baby!

Oh, what joy forgiveness had brought to my sweet sister Rachel and me, a warm rain drenching and satisfying our thirsty souls.

Jacob had sent waves of cattle, sheep, goats, donkeys, and camels as a representative of his desire to reconcile with Esau. To our surprise, the messengers came back in a rush, shouting, "Esau follows with four-hundred armed soldiers!"

Jacob ran ahead to plead before his brother. When he saw Esau, he bowed seven times. Esau dismounted at once and ran to scoop Jacob up into his arms. He would not let go of his brother. Whatever pain had built the wall between them crumbled before our eyes. It was evident.

Jacob was forgiven.

How Esau loved him! It was a beautiful scene unfolding before us in the desert land of Canaan. I would never forget seeing two grown men enfolding each other until they appeared as one, crying before their troops. They were not ashamed.

Esau told Jacob the sad news that their mother, Rebekah, died some years before. He and his father, Isaac, had buried her in the cave by Abraham and Sarah. Isaac still mourned her.

The brothers talked for hours. We heard their laughter but more than the sounds we heard, we saw their unity. They were at peace.

Esau rose to go. "Please allow me to leave one of my regiments behind to escort you safely through the desert to our father's home."

"Thank you my brother, but with our large caravan of family, servants, and livestock, we must move at our own pace. We make many stops along the way, but I thank you for your offer."

Esau had refused all the hundreds of livestock Jacob brought him. "You keep them, my brother, for I have quite enough." Why would a man refuse such generosity? But Jacob insisted so Esau took the gifts, and with all his warrior servants returned to his home in the desert near the Dead Sea.

Esau looked at his brother one last time. "Good-bye Jacob. We will meet again."

"Goodbye, Esau. Until then."

We continued our journey toward Isaac's home in Hebron.

Jacob grieved for his mother and wished he could have seen her again. Time would have to heal his heart. I was so glad Rachel and I had mended our relationship. With Esau's forgiveness, Jacob's family was at peace and he wore his contentment like a princely robe. Everything was perfect.

One day as we neared Bethlehem, still on our way to Isaac, our caravan came to an unexpected halt. Something was very wrong. I saw Jacob running, breathless, to my cart. He bent over to catch his breath so he could speak.

Frightened, I held my hand out to him. "Jacob, what's wrong?"

"Rachel… in terrible labor. Please come. You must…help her, Leah!"

I summoned the midwives, and then I ran to see my little sister racked with pain. Her body was writhing and distorted. So intense, these contractions, I doubted whether she would survive the delivery. It was too much. Her breathing was shallow and she gasped for air.

I wiped her forehead with cool, damp cloths. The midwives shook their heads with a silent message to me. "She will not live."

Rachel looked at me. She knew and accepted the truth. She would give her life for her son, and for the love of Jacob.

I kissed her cheek and whispered. "Rachel, if the worst happens, do not fear for this child or Joseph. I will cherish them as my own."

With the announcement from the women that she had a son, Rachel turned to Jacob. "Twelve sons for you." She squeezed my hand, called out, "Ben…oni…."

With that, my sister slipped away from us. Forever.

Jacob whispered, "I will call him Benjamin…favored son."

He turned, weeping, and walked to a quiet place. I swaddled Rachel's newborn, who now breathed with ease. I handed him to the midwife and went to find Jacob. I sat beside him, but did not speak. I knew he was numb from this tragic loss. Words would not help. His pain shook him to the core, leaving him as helpless as one of Rachel's little lambs.

At last, his hand reached for mine and he drew me close. He put his arm around me and we sobbed until there were no more tears.

He straightened. "Thank you, Leah, for being here…and… thank you… for your love. Both to me…and to Rachel."

I nodded. He spoke the truth for I had loved them both with passion.

"We are near Bethlehem—will you accompany me to bury her?"

"Of course."

"Tomorrow."

The next day, Jacob placed a big stone marker above Rachel's grave but along with the stone, he left his heart there too. As did I. He would love her until the day he died. And so would I.

We traveled on with the memory of our beloved Rachel following us. I held baby Benjamin and cared for him with tender affection, and Joseph sat between us. He held his brother's tiny hand.

We came at last to Hebron. What an occasion it was! Both Jacob and Isaac cried tears of agony and remorse because of the wasted years, choices made, blessings given, family pain, and all that had passed between them. Jacob held his father in his strong embrace. Isaac cupped Jacob's face in his feeble hands as tears invaded his face. "I thought I would never see my son's face again."

He rubbed Jacob's hair and touched his beard. Though he could not see clearly, he did not mistake which son he held this time.

Isaac welcomed me and delighted in meeting each of the twelve sons of Jacob and our daughter Dinah. One by one, he laid his quivering hand on every child's head and prayed a blessing.

We told him about our family during all the time Jacob had been in Haran.

My children were older now, freeing me to mother both Joseph and Benjamin. Jacob's spirit was peaceful and in harmony with my own. Joseph began to call me "Mama" and Benjamin mimicked with Ma-Ma. True to my word to Rachel, I loved them as my own.

Jacob adored his two sons from Rachel more than any of his other sons. Just as his mother Rebekah had favored him, he favored Joseph and Benjamin. It hurt, but I understood. They were the only part of Rachel he had left.

I thought about the forgiveness of Esau and the reconciliation of Rebekah's sons. How it would have blessed her to see that miracle in her family.

We lived two years in Hebron caring for Isaac and when he died, we sent a message to Esau. All the grandchildren thanked God they had known him, even if for a short time. It was a blessed sight as Esau and

Jacob, united in brotherhood, buried him. From these two sons had come twenty-four princes and one princess. The brothers laid their father to rest beside Rebekah, the love of his life, along with Abraham and Sarah, in the great tomb of Machpelah. Jacob looked at me. "Leah, you and I will be laid to rest here when we die." But Rachel was buried near Bethlehem.

Jacob inherited his father's vast estate, and I inherited two precious children from Rachel. I had Jacob to myself, except for the two handmaidens we had given him in our competition and jealously. I missed the sister of my youth. I grieved that she never knew Benjamin or lived to watch Joseph grow into a wonderful young man. And oh, she would have been so proud to see the love Jacob lavished on her sons, as he had lavished on her. I was able to see the beauty of their love and not be jealous.

Jacob became my friend and companion. I had lived so many days believing I wasn't loved enough, pretty enough, or good enough. I spent years chasing the one thing I would never have: Jacob's love. And yet, I had his friendship.

That was enough.

But as my days wore on, I found true joy when I saw I already had all I really needed: God's perfect love. For it was He who blessed me with my children. He who watched over me and protected me. He taught me to love Him the way I had loved Jacob.

The day came when I asked myself how much more of my life I would give away to unfulfilled expectations and shattered dreams.

On that day, my answer was, "No more." I surrendered my efforts to make Jacob—or anyone—love me. Instead, I focused on loving them.

And with the love that forgives, I was restored.

My life had been imperfect. But now, with God's love, I knew.

It was enough.

Read Leah's story in Genesis 29-33

CHAPTER 6
Rachel

WANDERING THROUGH THESE hills and valleys in Haran with my sheep, a love for the outdoors lived in me. Here I was most alive and free. The meadows provided a place for me to ponder, dream, and be contented. I was a shepherdess and I tended my father's sheep.

As the seasons changed, so did the landscape of the pastures. I took in every delicious pleasure while I watched my sheep. They were like little children. With someone watching over them, they were content. But without, they scattered and wandered everywhere. My sheep knew me and I knew them. If a sheep wandered away, I brought it back to the fold.

I rose early and led our flock to different pastures. The meadows called my name. Time passed quickly and the day was spent before I realized. I looked at the sun to see it was time to lead the flock to water. I reached for my staff and rose from my resting place. I began walking to the gate. This was a signal for them. The sheep stopped grazing, looked up, and followed me. I led them to the well, where I filled the troughs, allowing them to drink the cool, refreshing water. Finally, I returned them to the safety of the pens.

This day, though, something was different at the well. A stranger stood among the shepherds who waited with their sheep and goats. The shepherds seemed distracted from their normal routine of waiting for all our flocks to gather. For when we all arrived, several shepherds worked together to move the heavy stone that covered the well.

Who was this stranger and what were the other shepherds telling him?

I came closer. They pointed toward me and at once, he hurried to remove the heavy stone by himself. I was amazed at his strength, for in all my years here, I had never seen one man alone remove this stone. He began to fill the troughs to water my sheep.

Then, he came to me.

Who was this man? I shivered. He was no ordinary man, this one, for he had the bearing of a prince. Why would one such as this stop here and water my sheep?

I was speechless.

The sound of his voice drew me as he spoke my name.

"Rachel,"

So the shepherds had told him.

"I am Jacob, the son of Isaac and your Aunt Rebekah.

They had told him of my family too?

He looked straight into my eyes. "I came at my parents urging to spend some time with your family, if permitted."

He paused.

"Yes?" I knew he had something else to say.

"And one more thing…I have come to find a wife."

At this remark, my heart pounded in my ears.

The afternoon was overcast and cool, but my face flushed. The story of Aunt Rebekah flooded my thoughts. Was this well fostering yet another chapter in our family's history? If so, I welcomed the thought.

A wife for Jacob. What did he desire in a wife? My mind raced to imagine my future with him.

"Rachel."

I came back to the moment in time to see that the stranger seemed overjoyed. His face beamed and his ebony eyes penetrated mine. Before I could respond, he kissed me on the cheek. I touched my cheek to keep his affection there. Other than my family, no one had ever kissed my cheeks. Did he see me blush or could he sense the reactions his kiss had prompted?

I could not find my voice nor peel my eyes away. Water pooled around his eyes. He was not ashamed of his tears.

He no longer felt like a stranger, but rather like a relative restored to me. Perhaps even more than a relative! A prince of destiny stood before me, not knowing he had already captured my heart, which stirred without my permission.

I didn't resist.

The kiss. After his reaction, I didn't know whether to kiss him back. Since he had asked about staying with us, I smiled. "Wait here, Jacob. Let me put the sheep in the pen and then I will send my father to bring you to our home."

I ran to announce my news. "Father, Father! Your sister Rebekah's son, Jacob, is at the well! He desires to stay with us."

Father's eyes lit up. He dropped his tools and rushed to bring Jacob to our home. By the time they returned, they were already talking as friends, or as uncle to nephew. Father showed him where to wash and be refreshed from his journey.

"Father, what do you think of Jacob?"

"He feels like part of the family. I will gladly provide food and shelter for him as long as he desires."

"Did Jacob tell you he comes seeking his wife?"

My father's eyes shone. "What a fine young man, and, he is a close relative."

"I think he likes me."

"As beautiful as you are, my daughter, I have no doubts."

When Jacob returned, father introduced him to the rest of our family. "Here is my wife of many years and the mother of my children."

Jacob kissed her cheek. "Beloved Aunt."

This delighted mother. "Welcome to our home, Jacob."

Father indicated my older sister. "And here is Leah, my eldest daughter."

Jacob leaned in to kiss her cheek as he had mine. She blushed too.

Father grinned. "I believe you have already met my youngest daughter, Rachel?"

A smile broke across Jacob's face as he looked at me and then back to father. "Yes, at the well."

"You will meet my sons when they return from the fields."

"Uncle Laban, it is a blessing to be in the presence of family. I am grateful for your kindness and to the Lord God who watched over me on my journey, leading me safely to you."

Father put his arm around Jacob's shoulder. "Son, you are my flesh and blood, please stay with us as long as you desire."

"Thank you for your kindness. I will not be a burden."

I noticed Jacob came with but a few personal possessions. I could not imagine how heavy my load would be, if I were ever to take such a trip!

We reclined as Jacob told us of his journey and shared news of his mother and father. "They are well, except father's eyes are failing. My twin brother Esau has married two Hittite wives, and that displeased both mother and father. Fearing that I might do the same, they sent me here to choose a wife."

There. He had said it. Announced his intentions in front of my family. I looked down, not wanting to let the others see the joy those words brought.

Father leaned in. "Jacob, I have no doubt that you will find what you are seeking here. Does my sister Rebekah still retain her beauty?"

"Indeed, time has been kind to her and she is still most beautiful. Father loves her as much now as the day he first met her."

What a beautiful love story. A love that never wanes—oh, that I could be this blessed.

We talked until we sensed Jacob was tired from his long journey. Father showed him to a guest room.

I went to my room, but could not sleep. The dreams I had now far overshadowed my dreams in the meadows. If only I could be the one Jacob seeks.

Did that kiss mean as much to him as it did to me?

I tossed and turned. I closed my eyes but the only thing I could see was Jacob's face. At last, I slept, warmed by all these thoughts.

Jacob arose early and went to work in our fields. In the days ahead, I heard father tell mother his nephew was more helpful than the combined efforts of my brothers. Clearly, Father was impressed.

Every evening, when I came to the well, there was Jacob, waiting to water my sheep. We had many conversations and it was apparent, something special was developing between us. As the sheep drank their fill, so my soul was filled.

One day Jacob smiled at me. "Rachel, do you realize it's happening again? Just as it happened to my mother, here at this well, so it is with us, the weaving of our past, our futures, and our families together?"

"I realized it that first day, but waited in hopes you saw it too."

Life went on around us, but all we thought about was each other. My family grew to love and appreciate Jacob. He was indeed a blessing.

If my family did not know by now that we were in love, they were more blind than Isaac.

Finally, one day at the well, Jacob took my hands in his strong grip.

"Rachel, the first time I looked into your beautiful eyes, peering at me through those long, thick lashes, I knew you were the reason I came to this place. Your grace, your beauty, and lovely form draw me beyond what I ever imagined possible. Nothing will satisfy me until I have you for my wife."

I was stunned at his passionate words. I could not speak.

"Rachel, how do you feel about this?"

"As I sat in the meadows tending the sheep, I forever dreamed of having a husband and a friend like you. I asked myself. 'Would he be handsome, would he be tall, strong, and kind? Jacob, you fulfill everything I dreamed for in a husband. To think of spending the rest of our lives together—nothing could please me more!"

"Rachel, I have a plan. I must speak to your father." He took my hands again. "I believe I found you because you were chosen, not by me, but by God, for me. The peace I have about this love could only come from my God. You are chosen."

After one month, father and Jacob talked.

Father first, and oh, how crafty he was about it. Father did not realize I stood close enough to hear his exchange with Jacob.

But I did.

Father spoke as though he'd just made a discovery. "Jacob, you shouldn't be working for me for free just because you are a relative. Tell me what your wages should be."

Jacob nodded. "I am glad you asked, Laban, for I have something to say concerning this. I am in love with your daughter Rachel. If you allow me to marry her, I will work seven years as her dowry to you. As you know, my inheritance remains in Canaan where I will return someday. But for now…."

He held out his strong hands to convince Father of the sincere intention behind his solemn pledge.

My eyes were wet at such display.

Jacob's voice rang out. "I dedicate to you all the labor of my hands as a bride-price for Rachel."

An unbelievable dowry! This was the greatest expression of love I could imagine. Jacob's promise went far beyond any woman's worth. My legs trembled. How could I be worth this much?

Oh, Jacob, how you treasure me!

I was sure father was overcome with Jacob's offer, but true to his ungrateful self, he was unresponsive to the passion in Jacob's voice. He should have taken Jacob into his arms and said, "No, Jacob, seven years is too much. Come…let us talk of it further." And if not that, why couldn't Father at least show his gratitude, embrace him, and receive the pledge?

But no, not my father.

He brushed his hand forward. "Better to give her to you than any other man." His words devalued both Jacob's offer and me. But Jacob didn't react. I peeked at him and saw on his face that he was glad my father promised me to him.

They shook hands, thus sealing their covenant agreement.

I was betrothed! It was out in the open now and everyone in our village and beyond would hear about our story at the well.

Typically, heads of family clans arranged marriages to preserve wealth, form alliances, and produce offspring. The father of the bride received a dowry and, if it was enough, the betrothal commenced. Sometimes marriage arrangements were made when children were born, but no one had been successful in the bidding of my hand. Father would not hear of it before this. What's more, no such arrangement existed for Leah, who by custom had to marry first.

But seven years would be enough time for father to arrange something so she could marry before I did. And while love was not necessary in these arrangements, I was to have it all: Jacob's love, his loyalty, and his children.

Many, many children.

Being betrothed carried all the meaning and commitment of marriage, except for the physical part. This was reserved for the wedding tent. Not only could we not consummate our marriage before then, but if either of us broke the engagement, we would be charged with adultery.

One afternoon, as I walked with my betrothed to the well, I asked him if the time seemed too long until we could at last be married.

His smile lit up my heart. "Rachel, the days come and they go. I have made a covenant that I must honor. It is my gift to you. No time is too long to wait for a prize such as you."

"Jacob, how I love you."

"We will move to my home in Canaan when my contract is complete. First, I must make amends with my brother, Esau."

Jacob told me what happened in Hebron with his father, mother, and his twin brother Esau. Such deception seemed tragic. Never had anything like that happened in our family.

"So this is what caused you to run away from such an inheritance?"

Jacob nodded. "Esau vowed to kill me. My father bade me to go at once to Uncle Laban's and stay until Esau's wrath quieted and, he made me promise to take a wife from among his people. God led me directly to you, here at the well."

That explains why he came with so little....

I couldn't imagine Jacob being involved in such deception. I sensed the great lament he still bore. Why had his mother, my dear Aunt Rebekah, involved him in such a scheme? How could a parent show favoritism to one child while damaging another?

Jacob went on. "I had an encounter with the God of Abraham at Bethel during my flight here. I stopped that night to rest there and placed a stone under my head for a pillow. My grandfather Abraham had built an altar there on his way from Haran to his Land of Promise in Canaan.

It struck me that I was fleeing from my inheritance but he was coming to his."

"Please tell me more of your God."

"The Lord visited me there, saying. ' I am the Lord, the God of your grandfather Abraham, and the God of Isaac. I will give you and your descendants the land on which you are lying. Your descendants will be like the dust of the earth, and you will spread out to the West and to the East, to the North and to the South. All peoples on earth will be blessed through you and your offspring. I am with you and will watch over you wherever you go, and I will bring you back to this land. I will not leave you until I have done what I have promised you.'"

Such a wondrous promise from the God of our ancestors! Surely Jacob was a man among men, even in God's eyes. I rejoiced that I would be a part of God's great promise to Jacob.

Jacob smiled. "I made a vow to God there, telling Him if He would be with me and watch over me on this journey, give me food to eat, and clothes to wear so that I might one day return to my father's house, then He, and He only, would be my God."

He touched my face. "Rachel, clinging to God's covenant with me helps me keep my commitment to your father."

I understood. A covenant relationship was sacred.

And I was content in waiting.

The time for our wedding approached. My dream was so close I could barely stand it. Soon I would be a wife, and before long, a mother. I couldn't wait until our little ones were in my arms. Mother would be a wonderful grandmother, and Leah, the perfect aunt.

One problem still loomed, undiscussed. Leah had yet to marry. I prayed Father was working to find her a husband, but he never even spoke of it. Still, it was not my place to ask.

Before long, Mother began sewing my beautiful wedding dress. I sat by her side, stitching my bridal veil. I tried it on every day, putting it on display for all to see. It was a reminder that my dream was drawing near.

At first, Leah seemed as excited as I. But as the day of my wedding drew nearer, her countenance darkened. And when I tried on my veil, she no longer smiled. But I was not worried.

One evening Jacob pulled me aside.

"The time has come at last for us. I am going to speak to your father about our wedding at supper tonight."

That night, when we finished our meal. Mother, Leah, and I left the room. I was nervous. What if father didn't keep his word? No, I must not worry. We peered from behind the curtain.

Jacob stood. He looked right at father. "Laban, the time has passed, the dowry payment is completed within the terms of our contract, and it is time to give me Rachel as my wife."

Father continued eating. The pause was too long! Why did he not answer? He had everyone's attention now. He took a drink, wiped his lips, and nodded. "So it is Jacob. I will begin preparations for your wedding immediately."

There, he had said it and it would really be as he had said! I wished he hadn't scared me so with his reluctance, but that was father's way. He always kept us guessing.

Mother was as excited as if she were the bride herself. She had waited for father's permission to begin the final arrangements. Now, with his words, her joy overflowed. She stepped back in the room and went to Jacob, and put her arms around him. "You have been ever so patient, even more than I."

Was she crying? I know I was!

Without a beat, Jacob answered, "Oh, the years seem but as a day because of the love I have for Rachel."

No one could speak after Jacob's pronouncement. His words blessed our home, filling it—and me. Would I ever forget those endearing words?

My life was, indeed, perfection.

Our home turned into a bustling center as we all prepared for the wedding festival. Father's affirmation had set all this in motion. It would not be stopped by any act, except that of God, and why would He do such a thing? No, this celebration would be flawless.

Our legacy was beginning.

The house was immaculate, menus arranged and prepared by the servants and Leah, all under the watchful eye of mother. The wine storage was full, and guests had started to arrive. Those from far away came early, setting up tents on our property. Those nights were immersed with laughter and anticipation of the big day.

The night before the wedding, I sat with Leah. It would be our last night together here in Father's home. I would have a husband and my life would be rich and full. Leah was happy for me, but I knew it was bittersweet because of the closeness we would lose. We laughed about the upcoming events of the next day—and the matter understood by all but spoken by no one.

I took her hands in mine. "Leah, one day your wedding will come and I will be as helpful as you have been for me."

She shrugged as if not believing that day would ever come.

But I knew it would. For her as it had for me.

I awoke with fluttering in my stomach. It was the day of my wedding! I was so excited. I could not think of eating. I wanted the hours to pass quickly. I would not see Jacob until tonight, at the festivities.

I applied a mud mask to my face. I had to look radiant, for the wedding guests, the wedding party, and Jacob. I washed my hair and let it dry in the outdoor air. Mother and Leah helped me curl my hair. I soaked in warm water, infused with fragrant petals and drops of sweet oil. A gift from Leah. The aroma lingered in the air above my head. It was so calming—I stayed until my fingers were wrinkled. I applied lovely oils and lotions to my skin.

The music drifted into my room. The party had started. I looked at my reflection in the silver platter. My skin did glow. I re-pined my hair and pulled a curly tress over each ear. With a touch of charcoal around my eyes, red clay for my lips, lotus perfume, and mother's pearls on my neck, I was ready to step into my wedding gown. My hands were shaking. Mother and Leah came to help. Leah brought my veil from its perch where it had called for weeks. I lifted it high and twirled it in the air. It was the very symbol of giving myself to Jacob. I turned to let mother and Leah in on my moment. We all giggled. I took a deep breath, and placed it on my head.

There.

This was my day. The day.

We walked from my room outside to where the party was in a lively mode. All were gathered here for me and for Jacob. I relished every enchanted moment. The music changed and all eyes turned in our direction. Mother went first, then Leah. I drifted in on father's arm, my feet only just touching the ground. I stood veiled but I could still see. Though now shielded from Jacob by this curtain, I would see him tonight unveiled….

Father stood on a large stone and made a noise to get everyone's attention for all eyes were still fixed on me. Jacob came to stand by him as he welcomed our guests. "Friends and family, welcome to the marriage of my daughter to Jacob from the Land of Canaan. Please enjoy the food and wine. We are happy to have you join us in this celebration."

Applause, cheers, and whistling.

Toasts and blessings flooded the night as…one by one…guests raised a cup in tribute to our love and the uniting that would take place tonight, making us one. I blushed at the thought, but I was ready to belong to Jacob.

Body and soul.

I looked at him, standing among our guests, and wished his family could have come. He was so handsome in his new tunic. But he would see them soon enough, for in but a week, we would travel to his homeland and claim his inheritance. I would be with Aunt Rebekah and live all my days there with my husband.

The guests dined and danced for hours, and soon it was twilight. Everyone stayed on, so the servants refreshed the food and brought more wine. It was time for me to slip away to ready myself. I heard Jacob laugh in a peculiar way. He had already taken much wine, and thanks to father, he would have to be led, or maybe carried into the wedding tent!

I stood in my room in my wedding dress for a moment as my mind drifted to thoughts of Jacob waiting in the tent. I loved the tradition surrounding it, our cozy cocoon for the next week. Inside were my favorite lilies with their alluring fragrance. One oil candle would give just the right glow. The servants had placed food to nourish us for the days ahead: fruits, cakes, dried meats, nuts, cheese, and olives. There was fresh water for drinking or bathing and a few clothes.

The wedding week offered Jacob and me uninterrupted bonding, uniting of our spirits, and building a strong foundation for our future together.

I took off the veil and placed it in on the table outside my door. I slipped off my wedding dress and laid it on my bed. No need to hang it up for I would not need this bed tonight.

I changed into my new nightclothes and donned my beautiful robe. I sat on the bench and released my hair. The curls fell around my shoulders like a cloak. I closed my eyes envisioning the symphony of events that led us to this day. I knew that soon father would return for me, place my symbolic veil on my head, and lead me to Jacob.

Hurry, father, hurry.

I waited.

Mother must be with the last of the guests, but it seemed too long. My heart raced. It was not wise for me to go outside alone on this night.

Where was father? I couldn't hear Leah in her room. She must already be asleep. She had risen before dawn every day in orchestrating the events at our home. She had been a wonderful help, easing the work on mother. And every day she'd been at my side to take the worries of a bride from me.

I hoped father had not stayed giving instruction to Jacob. No, not on this important night. Something else was wrong! I pushed my dress aside and sat down hard upon my bed. My hands were ice cold and my stomach tied in knots.

I was helpless. I wanted to cry but my makeup needed to be fresh and beautiful for Jacob. Instead, I bit my nails.

My door opened at last but it was not father. It was mother who entered my room. She had been crying.

"Mother, what's wrong?"

"Rachel, I have something to tell you."

"Mother, what is going on? Has something happened to Jacob? Has he been stricken, or is he dead?"

My mother's sorrowful gaze was almost my undoing. "Your father has deceived Jacob tonight. He made him drunk and then put your veil on Leah and led her into your wedding tent."

I don't recall another word she uttered. Words didn't matter now, for the knife of betrayal had sunk deep into my heart. Better I had died than hear such news! I cried out. My stomach heaved. I wept until I had not another tear inside. At last, I lay exhausted on my bed—my tears staining my beautiful robe.

"Why?" Where was the God of Abraham, Isaac, and Jacob tonight? What of my destiny at the well?

Tonight I was the lost sheep, betrayed by my shepherd, who did not care for me and had not come to rescue me.

I was forever changed. The trust, faith, and dreams born in this home…

All were gone. They had died within me.

As had my heart.

Morning dawned when I heard Jacob's voice. He was sobbing my name.

I looked out to see him bent over, wailing as if receiving a death notice of a loved one.

And so he had…. he just didn't know it.

He held his head and wandered in a circle. "No, no. It cannot be! Please, God, no." He mumbled on about deceiving his poor blind father and his brother Esau. "Now I am the one deceived, for this is what I deserve."

I wanted to go to him. I moved in his direction, and he fell at my feet. He wrapped his arms around my ankles and drenched my feet with his tears. He begged with broken words. "Please… forgive me."

Father interrupted, looking down his nose at Jacob as though he were being foolish, as if his offense against my betrothed and I was but a minor breach. "Jacob, it is not the custom in our country to marry off the youngest daughter before the older. The eldest is always given first. What's done is done. Let Leah have her wedding week with you, and then I will give you Rachel. Of course for this you will serve me another seven years."

I couldn't speak. Like one of my tender lambs, I had been sacrificed by father's greed—he had killed my dreams using my veil as his weapon, in exchange for seven more years of Jacob's labor.

Jacob was begging now. "I will do whatever you ask…only give me Rachel."

"Seven years, Jacob."

As I turned away, Jacob spoke again in a low, raw voice. "Laban, you could have asked anything. I would have worked my entire life for Rachel."

My heart rejoiced on hearing these words.

Exhausted from the trauma and ruination of my wedding, at last I slept. Jacob went back to my wedding tent—to another woman.

My sister.

I stayed in my room and busied myself with all the chores waiting for me. I took all the time, seven days, as a matter of fact, packing up my hopes and dreams.

I would not need them now.

The week passed. I bathed, released my hair, put on my still unused nightgown. Had it only been a week? My past, present, and future ran together as I stood waiting again for father. Would he fail me again? Today I would be given to Jacob as his wife…his second in seven days.

The symbolic articles of my nuptials mocked me. A used veil, a tear stained robe, an occupied ceremony tent, and a defiled wedding bed. No, I would not need the veil, for I was already exposed. Even if I wanted it, it was not available.

I looked out of my room to see Leah leaving the tent, my veil in her hands. Though she did not know it, she carried something else…

My dreams.

I came to Jacob with nothing but my love and I felt his arms strong about me. In his presence, I did not doubt his love. I had never seen him happier, having me all to himself. There were moments I didn't obsess on the great offense to me. But, somewhere in my journey of grief and loss, I slipped away from Jacob, losing hope for my future.

Everything had been spoiled.

Never before had I doubted anyone, but now I questioned everyone. I held every offense inside, where they fueled my bitterness. I asked myself, over and over, where was my mother in all of this? How could she have let my beast of a father do this? How could my wicked sister have let it happen? Could not she have cried out?

And, the most important question of all…

Why didn't Jacob know it was not me?

Had he not told me he could paint my portrait even were I not present, because he held my face and my very form ever before him?

Yes, he had. Which left me with one, terrible conclusion…

Even he had betrayed me.

I grew to hate Leah, doubt Jacob, distrust my mother, detest my father, and abhor myself. I changed into someone I didn't know or like. Gone were the days of the innocent daydreams of this shepherdess. I demanded Jacob prove his love to me, to somehow make up or erase what had happened. This frustrated him to no end because we both knew that he could not rewrite the past.

I wanted something I could never have….to be his first and only wife. My what-ifs became my constant companions, but they could not change things. I could not move on and I could not find my way to forgive.

While I was lost in my roiling emotions, Leah became pregnant and bore a son to Jacob. They named him Rueben. For this, I tried to be happy. Before long, another son, Simeon. I held him and told her he was precious. The third she named Levi, and then a fourth, Judah.

Had my sister no mercy for my plight? Could she not see this was killing me?

No, it was obvious now. I would be shown no mercy. Life centered on her and the sons she bore, and in this, she delighted. Four in a row. Was this an act of God for some purpose yet unknown to me?

By now, my secret was revealed.

I was barren.

Angry with everyone, I now included Jacob's God in the circle of my betrayers. I hated Jacob because he couldn't give me a son, yet it never occurred to me that my bitterness was preventing me. Did he love Leah more now because of the sons of the promise, sons I thought were to be mine?

I went to Jacob. "Give me children, or I'll die!"

I was shocked when he raised his voice. "Am I God? He's the one who has kept you from having children!"

So I was being kept from motherhood. Did I have it within me to help my situation? Leah should not, and would not, be the only matriarch in this family. Not if I could do something about it.

And there was one thing....

I brought my handmaiden to Jacob, pleased that I had found a way. "Take Bilhah, and sleep with her. She will bear children for me and through her I can have a family, too."

So he slept with Bilhah, and she bore a son. I named him Dan and said, "God has vindicated me! He has heard my request and given me a son." But one was not enough.

To my good fortune, Bilhah gave Jacob a second son I named Naphtali. "For I have struggled hard with my sister, and I'm winning!" Leah four, me two...what was I thinking? That's not winning!

Leah, not to be outdone, turned our conflict into an all-out competition. Now discontent, she followed my lead and gave her handmaiden Zilpah to Jacob.

Now there were four wives for the man who only wanted one.

Zilpah gave him a seventh son. Leah named him Gad, and said, "How fortunate I am!" Then she gave another son, number eight, Leah named

Asher, for she said, "What joy is mine! Now the other women will celebrate with me."

I scoffed inside. What other women? Perhaps Bilhah or Zilpah, but not me!

Leah gave birth to another son, Issachar. Now nine sons. She bore yet another son she named Zebulun. "Now my husband will treat me with respect, for I have given him all these sons." There were now ten.

How many would be enough?

As many as it took me to win!

I couldn't take it anymore. I was more bitter and meaner than ever. There wasn't much heart left in me. I died a death every day with all the children being born around me. I tried to be happy for them and for Jacob, yet I was unfulfilled, still barren.

For fourteen years.

And then…

It happened!

Then God opened my womb. I was pregnant at last! I declared, "God has removed all my shame!" When I told Jacob, his joy was boundless. For the first time since the betrayal, I saw the man I had fallen in love with. And I saw his love for me, shining in his eyes.

A sound behind me drew my attention. Leah, standing nearby, turned and slipped away. She must have heard my words to Jacob. I waited to feel the victory…

It did not come.

Instead, in that moment God sent grief to pierce me. And something more.

Shame.

As I pressed my hands to my belly, over the place where my child grew, I saw as never before what I had done. Even as Jacob stole from his brother, had I not done the same? Had I not stolen from father, my husband, and my own beloved sister? And from myself? Did I not let bitterness take root within me, until all the years, the joy we could have had, were destroyed?

God showed me I had. I harbored contention and competition for the man we both loved. I caused a great chasm in my family when the only thing I ever wanted was something I already had…

Jacob's love…and now, his children. Now, only one thing hindered me.

I needed to forgive Leah.

Leah was not in her tent. She was in the garden. I heard great sounds of sorrow and remorse. I listened. She cried out to God to forgive her for withholding love and affection from me! She said she never knew I felt shamed until she heard my words, and knowing that had broken her heart. My heart softened to see her exposed in this way. She lay over the altar, heaving with great penitence. I came close and touched her. She turned to sit on the altar with me. I reached deep inside my heart. "Leah, will you forgive me for the bitterness I have shown you, my dear sister?" She could not contain her sobs. I kept on. "I was jealous of you for all the sons you bore to Jacob."

With this, she hugged me until I could scarcely breathe. I thought about the love and affection I withheld from her…all those years. I was surprised that I was the one freed by owning my sin. I was clean!

Leah was overjoyed, forgiving me in an instant. "Oh Rachel, I paraded my ability to have children in front of you like a banner of pride. I am so sorry." She dropped to her knees and begged my forgiveness but in that moment, I could not remember one offense she had done to me. Our embrace was the medicine I needed. The healing had begun in me, from the inside.

This miracle of healing and forgiveness changed me. My joy returned, and Jacob was delighted to see me happy again. As my stomach grew, so did my love grow for Jacob, Leah, and the child I carried. I tasted the sweet blessing a mother feels when her baby moves inside: stretching, kicking, and turning.

My life seemed perfect once again, bringing the day when I gave birth to our precious son. I had not expected an easy delivery. God blessed me as my family and the midwives gathered to help. When the announcement came, "You have a fine son…"

I cried. I was complete. No more sorrow and no more shame.

Jacob was thrilled at the birth of this son more than all his others.

I smiled at my husband. "I want to call him Joseph, 'Jehovah increases.'"

He agreed, acknowledging that this gift was directly from God. I placed Joseph in his father's arms. He raised him above his head, offering him to God as he prayed blessings, protection, and bounty upon him. With my motherhood established, a new bond began with my husband. I no longer felt like a failure. I was enough.

There were now eleven sons in Jacob's name, but I knew the truth…

Joseph was his favorite.

One day Jacob called Leah and me to the field where he was with his herds. He had never done this. It had to be something of great importance. "God has spoken to me saying I must go back to my homeland which He promised me, saying, 'I will be with you every step of the way.'"

While Jacob's own wealth was abundant because of his hard work and God's blessing, his efforts had also increased my father's wealth. And yet Father refused to release Jacob when all his years of service were completed.

Jacob said we would leave while father was gone to his distant pastures, overseeing the shearing of his sheep. He looked from me to Leah. "This would be the perfect time for us to leave, if you both agree."

I looked at Leah and spoke boldly. "Let us flee with our husband to preserve his wealth and our inheritance."

Leah turned to Jacob. "Then it is settled. We will go."

Retracing the steps of our great-uncle Abraham, who left here on the call from God, we also would go. I thought of Aunt Rebekah and her willing heart, how she left with Eliezer because of a prayer still perched on his lips and three words resting on hers: "I will go."

And now, because of God's voice in Jacob's ear, we would retrace the steps Jacob took when he fled for his life. We would cross the threshold of his inheritance.

Canaan.

In secret, we packed all we had acquired over the years. The servants loaded our many possessions. We were surprised to see how our wealth had increased. Finally, like a formation of birds in the skies, we took our early morning flight, commencing our mass exodus before the sun rose in Haran.

What I did not tell anyone was that I stole my father's idols. Although Father knew of the Living God, he still trusted these idols to guard his home and bestow blessings. I don't know why I took them…

Well, yes I do.

First, I didn't want Father consulting them for the direction of our pilgrimage so that he could find us and force us to return. Second, I wanted to remind him that he had withheld mine and Leah's dowry. But most of all…

I wanted revenge for what he had stolen from me. Now, he would feel the pain of losing something dear.

Jacob did not consult or worship idols, in fact, he detested them. He served only the True and Living God. But even knowing this, I clutched Father's precious idols in my grasp and smiled…

Now, we were even.

Father overtook us near the border of Gilead where we encamped. I was in my tent when I heard him arrive. I stayed inside, listening.

He yelled at Jacob. "What do you mean by stealing away like this? How dare you drag my daughters away like prisoners? Why did you slip away secretly? Why did you steal away? And why didn't you say you wanted to leave? I would have given you a farewell feast, with singing and music, accompanied by tambourines and harps. Why didn't you let me kiss my daughters and grandchildren and tell them good-bye? You have acted very foolishly!"

I waited for Jacob to reply, but Father didn't give him the chance.

"I could destroy you, Jacob, but the God of your father appeared to me last night and warned, 'Leave Jacob alone!' While I can understand your feeling that you must go, and your intense longing for your father's home, but why have you stolen my gods?'"

So many questions. So many accusations and so much anger. But I knew Father. All this show was mere chatter because all that mattered to him were the missing idols.

He took a breath at last, and Jacob had a chance to speak. "I rushed away because I was afraid. I feared you would take your daughters from me by force. But as for your gods, what have I to do with them? For you know I do not worship these! Now see if you can find them, and if you do, let the person who has taken them die!"

Fear seized me such as I had never known before! My husband had just pronounced a death sentence on me!

But Jacob was not finished. "And if you find anything, anything at all that belongs to you"— he spread his arm in a dramatic sweep over the perimeter of the camp. "Identify it before all these relatives, and I will give it back!"

I jumped up and found the idols, then placed them under a saddle perched on the floor. I sat on it, spread my dress over it, and determined I would not move until my father had gone.

Father searched every tent for his precious idols. I heard his voice outside. I was next. It was obvious he had yet to find anything.

He stepped inside. I looked up. "Please, Sir, forgive me if I don't get up for you. I am in the woman's way and cannot rise." He nodded and continued his search around me, in every bag and trunk, but he could not find his idols.

Now it was Jacob's turn to be angry. "Laban, what's my crime? What have I done wrong to make you chase after me as though I were a criminal? You have rummaged through everything I own. Now show me what you found that belongs to you! Set it out here in front of us." He spread his arms again. "Lay it out here before everyone to see and let them judge between us!"

Like an eruption of a dam, his words spewed forth, drenching father. "For twenty years I have been with you, caring for your flocks. In all that time your sheep and goats never miscarried. In all those years, I never used a single ram of yours for food. If any were attacked and killed by wild animals, I never showed you the carcass and asked you to reduce the count of your flock. No, I took the loss myself! You made me pay for every stolen animal, whether it was taken in broad daylight or in the dark of night. I worked for you through the scorching heat of the day and through cold and sleepless nights. Yes, for twenty years I slaved in your house! I worked for fourteen years earning your two daughters, and then six more years for my flock. And you changed my wages ten times! In fact, if the God of my father had not been on my side—the God of Abraham and the fearsome God of Isaac—you would have sent me away empty-handed. But God has seen your abuse and my hard work. That is why He appeared to you last night and rebuked you!"

Censured now in the condemnation of Jacob's truth, father countered. "Come, Jacob, let's make a covenant, you and I, as a witness not to harm each other in the future."

There he went again, acting as if he had done no wrong, just like on my wedding night!

Father continued. "The pile of stones in this place will stand as a witness to remind us of the covenant we make today. I will never pass this pile of stones to harm you, and you must never pass these stones or this monument to harm me. I call on the God of our ancestors—the God of your grandfather Abraham and the God of my grandfather Nahor—to serve as a judge between us."

So now he called upon the true and living God? Was it to please Jacob, or did he hope for mercy from the God he knew could destroy him in one moment?

No matter, Jacob took an oath before the fearsome God of his father Isaac, to respect the boundary line. He offered a sacrifice to God on the mountain and invited everyone to a covenant feast. We spent the night on the mountain.

The next morning, Father kissed all his grandchildren, Leah and me. He blessed us and departed.

And my secret was still hidden away.

Once inside Canaan, Jacob sent messengers ahead to tell Esau he was returning home. He divided all that he had brought and sent herd after herds, and gifts for Esau. Jacob separated his family in two groups, thinking if Esau and his soldiers decimated half, at least the other half of his family would be saved.

Jacob feared his brother's anger because of the awful wrong he had perpetrated on Esau. Like my husband's brother, I had known anger. Did Esau harbor bitterness as I had? What would he take in retaliation after all these years?

Jacob's life?

When the messengers returned, their report was alarming. I caught my breath as I listened.

"Jacob, we have seen your brother Esau. We told him of your journey home. He comes, riding with intention behind us with four hundred armed men!"

Jacob feared even more. Had not his peace offering been enough to right the wrong he had done?

We saw Esau coming in the distance. Jacob ran ahead, bowing seven times to the ground as his brother approached. But to our astonishment, Esau dismounted his camel and ran to Jacob. He was not angry at all. Rather quite the opposite. He threw his arms around Jacob's neck, embraced him, and kissed him.

The scene before us unfolded in slow motion as their tears flowed down their faces, a symbolic washing away of the rift between them.

This panorama would forever replay in my mind. The power of forgiveness healed yet again.

Esau looked at all the women and their children. "Who are these people with you Jacob?"

"These are my wives and the children God has given to me, your servant,"

"And what of all the flocks and herds I met as I came to meet you?"

"They are your gift, My Lord, to ensure your friendship. It is with joy I present you this division of all my property and livestock. I have earned these and brought them to you from the labor of my hands from the land of our dear mother."

"My brother, I do not require gifts, for I have plenty." A hush fell upon us as we listened. Still wiping his eyes with the backside of his wrists, Esau declared. "I have everything I need, more than enough, please keep it."

Jacob insisted, "No, if I have found favor with you, please accept these gifts from me." His voice broke as he finished. "And my brother, what a relief to see your friendly smile today. It is like seeing the very face of God!"

I didn't know about Esau but I knew how Jacob felt about seeing the face of God. Such a remarkable declaration. Esau relented at last to receive the gifts but only after his brother begged him.

Jacob inquired. "How is our father?"

"Our father is well. Although his sight is gone, he still remembers and asks of you whenever I visit him. I am sad in telling you that our mother has passed." Jacob fell to his knees, sobbing once again. Esau knelt by him, arms tight around his shoulders.

At last they stood. Another tender embrace and Esau departed for his home in Seir that same day. Such an amazing and redemptive story I observed. I would relay it to my children in hopes of helping them live at peace with each other. Heaven knew they needed it.

To know Esau was content and no longer bitter was beyond the realm of my understanding. Wasn't brotherhood about preserving all their wealth, gaining more than the other, and hoarding it for their heirs? But Esau seemed not keep such a record, either of offenses or of the numbers of his herd. It was uncomplicated, the reunion I had witnessed. All was forgiven, all forgotten, and all restored. Peace had come at last between my husband and his brother.

Just as it had for my sister and me.

Why did I take those stupid idols! Jacob's oath to my father haunted me: "The one who took them will not live!"

God…help me!

God spoke again to Jacob: "Move on to Bethel and settle there until it is time for you to receive your inheritance. Build an altar and get rid of the idols among you. Purify yourselves and put on clean clothes."

So we were going to Jacob's oasis, where God visited him as he fled from Esau. Soon we would experience Bethel, the very place where God made His promise and where Jacob made his covenant to God.

But before we could go to Bethel, we had to deal with those foreign gods and idols. We knew what purification meant. It was time to give our attention back to God, the One, True, and Living God.

I welcomed this.

So the servants, handmaidens, and I surrendered the idols without regret. Many of us were accustomed to wearing gold earrings as a symbol of good luck. In making our renewed commitment, and to show our desire to please God, we gave these as an offering as well, even though not we were not required to do so.

Jacob buried everything there.

When we came to Bethel, he built onto the altar, prayed, and celebrated with God. It was Holy Ground. The Lord renewed his promise to Jacob and changed his name to Israel! So much of his life had been in conflict with the men in his life: his father, his brother Esau, and my father Laban. But now those days were behind him, and he would do work with the Lord God as "Israel."

Prince with God.

He said when God changed a name it sealed a covenant. Just as Abram became Abraham and Sarai became Sarah, so Jacob was now Israel.

My life was taking a new turn now that I surrendered those idols. I treasured every day. Being clean opened the doorway to joys I never knew. I could hardly wait to find Leah and tell her my news. I was pregnant again! She cried as she held me and told me she was happy for me, and for the child that would please Jacob so much. "I hope to make it to Hebron and meet Jacob's father Isaac before the baby comes."

I smiled. "I hope it's a boy!

"Me, too Rachel. This will give Israel twelve sons of promise!"

News reached us that Isaac was not doing well. Jacob pulled up our roots in Bethel and prepared to move to Hebron, where he would care for his father.

Jacob would receive his inheritance at last.

We neared Bethlehem on the last leg of our journey and the great reunion with Isaac.

I was sorry I would not meet Rebekah. She would have loved our Joseph and the chance to cradle the new baby I would soon birth. Neither would she embrace her beloved Jacob…for it was not to be. The last time she saw him, his back was to her as he came to us. Now that he was returning, she was not there.

As we neared Ephrath, I was besieged with unbearable pain. But it was not time for my delivery! I cried out for Leah. Jacob stopped our cart and went for her. She would know what to do. She brought the midwives, who tried without success to ease my trauma. This was different than when I birthed Joseph. I knew…

Something was wrong.

I could see panic in the eyes of those around me. Had not these friends and family witnessed the birthing of eleven sons and one daughter in our family already…all without such disturbance?

I focused on Leah, which brought a measure of calm even though excruciating pain still wracked my body. She placed cool cloths on my head and held my hand. She wiped my brow, and I felt again all the pain of unforgiveness released, wiped away with her strokes of love.

She bent down to whisper to me. "Rachel, I will take care of Joseph and this baby too. I will treat them as my own, because of my love for you, my precious sister. Do not fear."

I could not bear the forceful pain as each stab stole life from me. The midwives announced I was birthing another son. Twelve sons for Israel—this completed his dream, but I knew I would not be able to share it with him.

In all the fear and trauma surrounding me, a sudden peace overcame me, and again, I knew.

That I was about to meet the God of Abraham and Isaac. The God who loved me.

The look of overwhelming loss in Jacob's eyes reached me, and I breathed a prayer to God to fill the void my passing would bring.

At last, I came to know…my husband *had* loved me best.

My breathing slowed.

I struggled for breath. This child would cost my life.

I didn't hesitate for one second.

With my last breaths, I called out "Ben...oni...'Son of my pain.'"

As everything faded, I heard Jacob whisper, "I will call him Benjamin—favored son…of my right hand."

My last breath escaped…and I slipped into the loving arms of my God.

Read Rachel's Story in Genesis 29-35

CHAPTER 7
Tamar

ANOTHER DEAD HUSBAND.

I heard a thud as Onan's body rolled onto the floor.

Heart pounding, I sat up and looked over the edge of our bed. There he was, lying flat on his back. He was not moving, not breathing, and not uttering a sound. His eyes were glazed, staring at the ceiling.

He was dead.

I ran out of our tent, dressed only in my nightclothes. The sun had just set. I scanned the area, searching for Judah…

Must find him…must tell him first.

Looking into his tent, I observed only Judah's wife Beulah saying nightly prayers to her idols. Judah was not there. I ran to the garden, but he was not there. My eyes searched the field—

There. I saw him.

The posture of a man still mourning the loss of his firstborn.

With my soul distressed and my heart aching for Judah, I approached. The news I bore would shatter him, with grief beyond what I could imagine.

"Tamar."

My heart pounded as if it would burst. "Judah, your son Onan"—how could I say it? How could I not?—"is dead."

He stared, pausing for a moment as if to absorb what he'd just heard. Then his body slumped. He grabbed his garment and rent it. He dropped to his knees and scooped up two large fists full of dirt, then tossed it in the air to let it settle over his body. Time and time again, he did this. Tears flowing down like a river mingled with the dust, forming droplets of mud, which stained his garment further.

And then He cried out. "My God, My God. What…do You want from me?"

The time of mourning for Onan passed. I sat, reflecting. Would I tell them about that night and what Onan had done? How he'd defiled the marriage bed, preventing me from even the chance of an heir….

Not just one, but two sons of Judah, both having been my husbands, were now dead.

No, I would not tell.

Judah would have to make a decision soon. I took my daily walk in the gardens, but a sense of foreboding settled upon me, so I cut my walk short. I entered Judah's home—

That's when I heard it.

Beulah was in distress. Again.

"Judah, send this girl away! Every time I look at Tamar, I am reminded of our dead sons and I cry. I see her and it brings back everything: sadness, sorrow, and heartache. I tell you, I cannot stand it. These feelings haunt me. Must I mourn forever? You must remove her from our presence."

I closed my eyes. *Speak, Judah….*

"Beulah, my heart still grieves too but…I am bound to the law of my fathers. I cannot send Tamar away without a promise…or an heir. She is to remain in my house forever unless I set her free to marry another. I must fulfill my duty to give her heirs, who will bear my sons' names, or promise her our only remaining son, Shelah, when he is old enough."

"Then, set her free!"

I held my breath, waiting for Judah to determine my fate.

"Very well, my wife, if it pleases you, I will not perform my duty unto her, but rather will send her back to her father's house as a widow, telling her to wait until Shelah is older. This will quiet her for awhile, but I commit to you, she will never be Shelah's wife."

So. It was done. I was betrayed.

Back in my room, their conversation rang in my ears. I knew three things from their conversation: I would not be allowed a husband from the house of Judah. I would be banished back to my father's home, a widow in mourning forever. And I was pledged to a husband that would never claim me.

Heavy footsteps sounded by my door—Judah. It had to be. My guess was confirmed when he stepped into my room.

"Tamar, go back to the house of your father and live the widow's life until Shelah is old enough. Then I will send for you and bring you again to my house where you can bear children with him. Take with you all the gifts I have given you and the other things you have acquired in my home. I have prepared servants to assist you and a camel to carry you."

What choice did I have? "Lord Judah." Though I acknowledged his message, I knew the words were from the mouth of a deceiver.

The room was silent, but for the long breath he exhaled. How relieved he was. Or was it a sigh of regret for the decree he had handed me?

Judah spoke no more.

It was done.

I gathered my things and left Judah's house, wearing widow's clothes. My journey home brought my mind to confusion and despair. Beulah suffered over the loss of her sons. I understood her pain. I came to Judah's home with high hopes, but also with a deep warning in my soul. Now, on my journey home, I laid to rest the hope that once welled within me. I came wanting to find the God of Judah, the One and only true God. But today...

I left knowing God's judgment had visited the house of Judah.

I relived the events of that dreadful night. Amid the chaos saturating the room where we lived, I stood, a frightened wife...with my husband dead on the floor, I cried out to the God of Abraham. Had not all of Canaan heard of the God who defended His own? My family's idols had brought me nothing but stone-cold stares—no presence, no comfort, and no voice. They could not help me.

I felt a presence. One that could only be that of the Lord God. His powerful presence comforted me, resting on me like a robe. He would help me. I trusted in Him that night.

I would trust Him now.

Although Judah offered servants and a camel for my journey home, I declined. His Beulah was not the only one who wanted to be alone. Now it was my turn. With a donkey carrying my possessions, I walked back down the dusty road, recalling all I'd been told of the family of Judah.

Father told me how the Hebrew, Judah, born unto his father Jacob and his wife Leah, moved into our region. "He had not yet taken a wife when he left his father's home in Hebron. No one knew why he distanced himself and came alone to Adullam. He soon became friends with Hirah, one of our village leaders. The elders welcomed Judah, for he had wealth and a family history that peaked everyone's curiosity. Soon, he took a wife—the daughter of Shua."

Tales followed Judah and his family until everyone knew his story, of his wealth and influence in his clan. But the most important thing about him was that he was highly favored and blessed by the Lord God, the God of the Israelites.

Through the years, his herds multiplied at an astounding rate, making him the wealthiest and most powerful man in our village. Judah and his wife Beulah had three sons, Er, Onan, and the youngest, Shelah. When people spoke of Judah, they did so with reverence—and even fear—because of the favor of his God.

I looked down to the dusty road, my mind still immersed in the life from which I was now banished. Who of our city's elders had known that I, of all the girls in Adullam, would become a member of the great house of Judah? Yet now, here I was—sent away. Even worse, sentenced to remain in widow's clothes, awaiting a call we both knew would never come.

I reached the road leading to my childhood home. It looked different. A new dignity rested upon the scene but I sensed the same love seeping out to embrace me, welcome me. The dowry from Judah had enabled my father to add more beauty and comfort to his home. A new gate with an arch, covered with profuse blossoms of passion vine, opened to a rose garden in full bloom, adding a delicious fragrance by our door. Although these outside beauties must have given my mother pleasure, I knew she had not changed. She would be as I had left her...forever caring, forever loving.

I placed my hand on the door that framed their enlarged and updated home. Memories of the day that first brought Judah to our door now invaded my mind. I withdrew my hand and sat on the step, for mother was not home.

I closed my eyes...and let the memories come.

My first memory of Judah was his ring. How it had glowed in the sunlight! The signet he wore on a cord around his neck was that of the man known as The Israelite. The ring and staff bore his signature and were as much a part of Judah as the clothes he wore. The staff he carried was not for stability, but rather for nobility. He was, in every way…a man of prominence.

A need brought him to our door that day. He came to do business with my father. Mother took my hand as we listened from inside.

"I am here to discuss your daughter Tamar as a wife for my son Er."

Father was quick. "Considering your standing in our community, I could not ask for a more qualified family."

Father, think! Not the wicked Er! Even you have labeled him as such—worthless *and* wicked.

"Because of your daughter's beauty and courage, I know she is a woman of worth and I very much desire to have her in my family."

Father did not speak, so Judah continued. "I have prepared, for your consideration, a dowry most deserving of Tamar. It is signed and sealed by my signet."

"Judah, I appreciate the words you speak of Tamar. She is of great worth to me. Let us talk further. Come in and sit. My wife will bring a drink for us."

As mother hurried to do Father's bidding, I stepped to the curtain.

Judah sat, but not before delivering a bold announcement: "I hold in my hand a deed to one of my vineyards. It boasts two hundred productive vines and adjacent to it, one hundred date palm trees. If acceptable to you, for the bride-price of Tamar, this property is yours."

Date palm…were not those words the very meaning of my name, Tamar? Did he know?

My knees grew weak, but not from his reference to date palms. Indeed, no. The weakness came from the thought of being married to his wicked son Er. Everyone knew. Judah was a man of character… but Er?

Say *no* father!

Mother squeezed my hand. I looked into her eyes and saw my fear reflected there.

But I knew the truth. Father was already thinking about herds, flocks, land, and wealth. This was a business arrangement, the best of his lifetime.

"Judah, you are the first to offer a dowry worthy of my daughter."

"There is but one stipulation. By accepting this offer, Tamar must make haste and wed my son as soon as possible. My household will plan every detail and host the wedding."

Father must have been speechless, for no words came forth.

"And, do not worry concerning the wine, for I possess the finest wines of our region."

My mind raced. Judah thinks this much of me? Never, in our village, had a bride received a dowry of this magnitude. But, to marry Er?

Father found his voice at last. "Very well, Judah. It will be as you have said. I will give Tamar as a bride to your son Er."

"I have delivered you the deed to the property." With those words, Judah departed.

And my fate was sealed.

I waited until Judah was gone, then stepped from the curtain shield to face my father.

He looked at me. "You heard?"

"Yes, Father. I am glad you will be rewarded generously. Yet…

"Yet?"

"Do you overlook the reputation of the Hebrew's son because of the bride-price?"

"Daughter, this is an offer I cannot refuse. Think of it, your mother and I will never want again. This will bring us comfort in our old age."

"But from your very lips you said one word describes Er best."

He inclined his head. "'Wicked.' And yet, Tamar, you do not see what your father sees. With your beauty, spirit, and determination, if any woman can subdue this man, it is you, my daughter."

"But Father, what of love?"

"Tamar, love is a dream for which you must wait. You have been to us all we ever wanted. I am releasing you to the house of Judah with enough love to sustain you. Under his covering, despite his wicked son, you will receive honor, provision, and the protection you deserve for the rest of your life."

He was not through. "All the joy, music, and laughter you have brought here, you will carry with you as a blessing to your new home. And, if all goes well, you will have many sons to secure forever your link to the house of Judah."

Such tender affirmation I could not refuse. I leaned into his shoulder. Perhaps father knew best. And yet, I could not hold back one last plea. "I have no choice?"

"Tamar, it is done. See?" He held up the document. "I have this promise sealed by Judah's signet. It will never be broken." He smiled. "And daughter, knowing Judah, this wedding will be the greatest festival Adullam has ever seen. We must hasten to invite all our friends."

Mother brought out all the pieces of cloth from her collection, spreading them out with pride on my bed. She extended her graceful hand, to sweep over them like a rainbow, inviting me to pick my favorite. The colors and textures were just like my mother, soft and beautiful. She waited to see which I would choose.

I picked up each piece and looked to see her face light up as she announced when and where she acquired them. At one, a smile started and spread from ear to ear. I knew it held a special story. It was the one. "Mother, I love this one the best."

She did too. "My daughter, I had this very occasion in mind when I purchased it long ago."

I treasured our last days together as she cut, measured, and sewed the linen gown for me. Each stitch was one of love. I worked alongside her as she showed me how to tat lace for the sleeves. It was a royal gown, one I would wear with honor, feeling all her love wrapping me. I was her beloved daughter.

"Tamar, you will find your delight in the care of your home and in the children you bear. A wife makes life easier for those in her care." This had been mother's quest, denying herself for the sake of her family.

Another day she recounted stories of her early days with father. She told about my birth, their only child, when perhaps father had hoped for a son…though he never said. She shared about their life together, the hardships, and certain sorrows that had brought them to this joyous time, with me at the center.

"You are prepared to be a bride, Tamar. In time, you will forget you were ever concerned."

I looked into her eyes. The years of dedication and hard work weighed heavy on her, but with Judah's bride-price for me, life would no longer be so harsh. Father was right to accept Judah's gift.

For this, if nothing else, I was grateful.

I gathered the things to take with me to my new home. Not much, just a few colorful scarves, dresses, and sandals that lay across my bed, ready to pack. I looked at the bed of my youth. Tonight would be my last night here in this room and this house, for I would forever remain in the house of Judah.

I reached for the brush from my childhood. Mother was watching. I knew what she was thinking, but I didn't speak to it. Instead, I reached for the pouch of combs, hair picks, and clasps needed for my long dark hair. A tear rested on my lashes.

Mother stood in the doorway. "You are lucky, Tamar, for your hair still falls in waves as you release the pins. Just like when you were a little girl."

"Oh, Mother." I reached for her and held her close as I shed tears, some for joy, some for concern, and some…well, just because.

"Tamar, you are beautiful, inside and out. Your children will bear your beauty as well. Although I grieve to see you go, I cannot wait to cradle your little ones in my arms."

With this, she turned and went into the other room.

I dabbed at my eyes. Mother would miss me. I had been a great help to her.

She returned cradling an idol in her arms. "Take this."

I could not. Was not Judah devoted to his God, apart from all others? What would he say if I brought this idol into his home? I covered my mother's hand with my own. "Not now, Mother. If need be, I will come back to retrieve your gift."

"But it will bring you blessings and guarantee fertility for you in the house of Judah."

"But Judah does not worship idols."

"Did not he permit his Canaanite wife to bring her household gods into his home?"

Though that was true, I declined her loving offer just the same.

I wanted to know more about The God of Judah. The One who never slept or slumbered, unseen yet wielding the power of protection over His own. If Er lived up to his reputation...

I would need the help of this God.

I paused. What if the time came when I had to make a choice between mother's gods and the God of the Hebrews? I knew about her gods. They had never moved or spoken from their sacred position in our home. And, as far as I knew, none had ever performed a miracle.

But I had heard the stories of the God of the Hebrews, of His favor and His protection—believers and non-believers alike saw evidence of His power. Who could escape His wrath, or His blessing? These stories reverberated throughout the region, creating fear not only of Him...but also of His children, "The chosen."

I had heard often of the powerful Abraham and his men, who defeated many kings. How Abraham's God went before him delivering his people in war, famine, and desolation. Then there was the horror of Sodom and Gomorrah. Fire rained down from heaven, wiping the city from the face of the earth. These stories brought a warning: Do not harm the chosen ones of the Lord God."

Our idols could never stand against this God. We bowed low on a rug in front of our gods, but Judah's God was ever-present, everywhere!

No, I would not take the idol into Judah's home. But I also would not choose now between Judah's God and my mother's. Instead, I would attend to the details of my wedding.

I awakened. It was my wedding day. Mother came to help me dress. I posed, and she cupped her hands to her mouth. She didn't need words—the glow on her face told me of the pride swelling within her.

Judah's cart arrived to take her to the celebration. Father and I would come behind them. She would walk into the festival looking every bit the queen, whose princess daughter would take a groom, a prince.

Father walked beside me, leading his donkey to the house of Judah. As I dismounted, Judah came. He held a beautiful ivory box in his hands. Looking at me, he caught his breath and handed me the box. "Tamar, you are lovely today, a radiant bride."

I heard only sincerity in his voice.

"This is a special day as I welcome you into my family. I have collected these wedding gifts just for you."

I opened the box to see bracelets, necklaces, rings, and earrings. I slipped a gold bracelet on each arm and put on the ruby earrings.

He smiled.

I was ready.

The party was more than I had imagined! Such a grand banquet, attended by Judah's many servants. Guests crowded the estate grounds, where he staged the festivities. It was indeed a feast to be remembered with music, dancing, food, and wine. Everyone was happy.

I looked around, but did not see my groom.

His father went to find him.

Er came back with Judah, but it was obvious he had already partaken of the wine and, commenced his celebrating early. He was magnificent. I had never been close enough to see his features. His face seemed chiseled, eyes round and dark. He was tall, the very image of Judah. Together, we made a stunning couple.

But when he spoke, his words showed his magnificence was only on the surface. "Let's get this thing over."

Not the words I longed to hear on my wedding day.

We danced, but his eyes were not on me. Something or someone else had caught his attention. This was just another ordinary day to him.

As tradition, Er and I entered the wedding tent and the crowd cheered. This was the final act of the celebration, the moment for which they came, for when we emerged—we would be husband and wife.

I entered married life as young and innocent as Er was handsome and arrogant. He bore a spectacular manner and when he talked, his melodic voice lured me. He knew how to charm, but he knew also how to diminish.

I knew within the first week, the very wedding week in the tent, that there was darkness in my husband. His mother spoiled him, and Judah was distant. I wanted to keep peace, but Er had no good words for anyone. Still, I clutched the dreams of subduing, molding, and shaping his character. I trusted the words of my father, "love might blossom and grow." Surely children would help this probability.

But the word—that one word describing him best—kept coming to haunt my mind.

Wicked.

When we moved out of the wedding tent and into Judah's home, Er's mother gave me a tour of their palatial estate. I noticed a small room beside her bedroom, near the great dining hall. I peered inside to see a table, with a rug before it, holding her idols. She pointed, naming them all, as if I didn't know.

Did Judah worship here? If not, where did he worship his God? I would ask him someday.

Judah's home had many rooms. A large, decorated chamber overlooking the gardens was given to Er and me. It was larger than the four rooms of my home put together! I sat on a bench by the window, gazing out over the many pastures, orchards, and vineyards. I would live a life of privilege here. I unpacked my few treasures and hung up my wedding gown, a reminder of my mother's love.

My husband had no desire to work or help his father. He did not go to the fields or gardens—neither did he help with the livestock. But he did have a routine. He frolicked and wasted his time and money carousing with his friends.

Er left for days without telling me. I would awaken in the middle of the night or in the morning hours to find him gone. Judah never spoke of his son's absence, and his mother acted as if this was normal behavior.

"Er will settle down soon, especially, when you have a child."

I wished I could be as certain as she.

One day I walked by the idol room to hear Er's mother pray before her deities. She asked for an heir, and I heard such agony in her words. Every month I hoped for the confirmation of pregnancy, and every time was disappointed. Having a child would not only assure the continuance of the family bloodline through Er, but would endear me to my new family.

I learned to shield my sorrow. The gods of Beulah had done nothing for me. I sat alone in the garden, imagining the protector and provider, the God of Judah. Did He see me? Did He have a child for me?

At meal times, I asked Judah questions about his family, all the way back to his great grandfather Abraham. "How did his family come to know the Lord God and be blessed by Him?"

Beulah left the room when Judah reflected on his past, and the boys disappeared at every mention of Judah's God, leaving me alone with him. A door was opening between us. Judah spoke of the relationship of his ancestors to the Awesome God. I sensed a rekindling, a tenderness. He began to speak of his mother, Leah, and his father, Jacob, and his many brothers. He said jealously and discord in his family had driven him from Hebron.

I sensed, though, that speaking of the past still grieved him. For as often as not, he would bring his words to an abrupt end, and leave the room.

I understood. For all that my new home was a place of wealth and opulence, I longed for the quiet love I once knew. And with each passing day…

I missed it more.

It was spring, the time for the yearly sheep shearing festival at Timnah. Judah, Er, and Onan set out with Judah's friend, Hirah, to go up with their flocks. I knew why the boys wanted to go. It was tradition for the men to celebrate the blessing of their herds. Many men engaged in the pagan custom with shrine prostitutes, who served in the temple. The sheering and lively celebration would last more than a week. The men packed their garments, tents, and supplies. They were jovial and their conversations were merry. They were ready to go.

Er's mother stood in the doorway by me. We waved good-bye and watched them leave.

On the fourth day, I was at my favorite spot in the garden when I looked up to see someone running in the distance. It was Judah. Hirah and Onan were with him. But Er…Er was not.

Something was wrong.

Hirah called out to me. "Tamar, bring Beulah to the great room! We bring dreadful news."

I went to find her, dread building within me. Why was my husband not with his father and brothers? Why had they come back so soon?

I found Beulah resting in her room. I touched her shoulder. "Judah is here."

She jerked to a sitting position, blinking and frowning at me. "What did you say?"

"Judah is here."

"No, it cannot be, unless, unless…something has happened. What is it Tamar?"

"I know not, but only that Judah bears great sadness. Come with me now as we take this news together."

I guided her down the hall. We sat on the bench in the great room. Hirah knelt by Judah, who sat on the floor with his face in his hands. He was sobbing.

Onan did not sit.

Beulah looked at Judah, and then shrieked. "Where is Er? What has happened to my son?"

"Please Beulah. Let me… start from the beginning." But he could not continue.

Hirah took up the tale. "The boys went to the temple with their friends, as they had every day. There was much drinking and celebrating as there always is…but in the night, Onan returned to us in the shearing fields and announced, 'Er is dead!'"

Beulah gasped and dropped to her knees. Her grief resonated through the quiet room, and chills raced down my spine.

Beulah wailed the question I could not. "How, how?"

Onan spoke over Judah, who still struggled to speak. And when he did so...he grinned. "He died in the arms of a temple prostitute!"

To see Onan gloat at revealing such news to his mother, with no concern, shocked me. How he took delight in announcing such horrific news! This was an evil act from an evil man. Er must have been a disappointment to his parents, but they did not deserve such cruel treatment from Onan.

At this, I stood. Judah had Hirah to comfort him. I went to Beulah. Though I could bring no tears of my own for Er, I stepped close and put my arms around his mother. I would honor the grief this news brought her.

The house of Judah plunged at once into mourning.

But Onan had already sneaked out the door and headed back to the festival, without a word of sorrow, condolence, or comfort to his mother or father.

Just like that, I was a widow. I retreated to my room to put on dark clothes and a veil. But inside I rejoiced, for I was free. Free of Er's wickedness, cursing, blasphemy, and vileness. Free of his godless ways. I had carried all these burdens alone. For me, my whole marriage had been a time of mourning.

I had already shed enough tears.

But no sooner did I rejoice than a realization came over me: I was subject to the Levir law. The brother-in-law rule! And my rejoicing changed to fear.

My only hope was that Judah would not invoke the law, for if he did, I would be subjected to Onan!

Er had been wicked but Onan...

He was a cruel and evil man.

After the required mourning period, Judah called Onan and me together. "My son, you must fulfill the Levir law for your brother Er to provide an heir in his name, who will share in my inheritance and care for his mother, Tamar."

Onan was furious. Words dripped from his mouth like poison. "How dare you command me to carry out this so called duty!'"

"You will perform your duty to your dead brother or leave this house with nothing!"

Judah's response shocked me. I had never heard him speak words of rebuke to any one in his home. But Judah was determined.

This union required no ceremony or festival. Rather, we would go into the wedding tent for one purpose: an heir for Er. And perhaps, an heir for Onan.

But Onan had other plans.

With his hands gripping my arms, he sat me on the side of the bed. "Regardless of what my father has sanctioned, you must understand that Shelah and I alone will share our father's wealth. Neither you, nor any child of yours, will get a scrap of the inheritance."

"But Onan, for your brother's sake…"

"Never!"

So violent was his vow, that I wondered…had he also fostered a way to eliminate Shelah and have all the wealth himself?

"Tamar, you may have our family's name, but never, ever my seed!"

His declaration rang out like an edict from the ruler of a kingdom. His kingdom.

True to his word, that night he used me for his pleasure but turned away to spill his seed on the ground. Such an act was blasphemy, and I turned from him, weeping that he had made me part of it.

As I wept, I prayed to Judah's God, begging Him to deliver me from this evil man. For I knew He was the only one who could.

I was startled from sleep by a thunderous crash.

I jerked upright, looking around the room, only to realize Onan was not beside me. Instead…his body lay still…on the floor. I jumped from the bed and knelt to place my hand to his mouth. I felt no breath.

He was dead.

I felt no sorrow. No fear. Instead, I knew this was judgment from Judah's God. I had prayed to Him for deliverance and it came swift.

And final.

I shifted on the step, pulling my thoughts from the past. Onan's death had freed me. But it also imprisoned me in my current situation. And so here I sat, alone, at my father's house, waiting for Judah to send for me to wed his remaining son.

But, the call didn't come. Judah's words to Beulah ran in my ears: "She will never, ever, marry Shelah."

I no longer bowed to my family's idols. They were empty works of man's hands. And I had experienced the hand of The Living God.

I was still under the covering and house of Judah, whose God was the Lord God. I had seen the severe hand of this mighty God. He had delivered me from two wicked and evil men.

In my heart, I sensed His presence. It comforted me, giving me hope. My future was at rest in His hands. I would trust Him…

And only Him.

Time passed and Father came with the news from the city. "Judah's wife has died."

Another tragedy in the house of Judah. Everyone saw that Shelah had come of age, but Judah would not fulfill his promise to me.

Even so, I knew there was a reason I was chosen and placed within the family of Judah. I knew it was to bear children in the name of Judah's house. It was my right and, unless I acted, it would not happen.

And so once more, I prayed to the One true God for help. And when my answer came…

I did not hesitate.

It was springtime. Judah always went up to Timnah for the annual shearing sheep festival. All the other men had already left the village, and Judah, as always, would be one of the last to leave.

My spirit confirmed within me. "I will carry out God's plan to fulfill my right to bear a child from Judah."

I would deceive Judah by playing on his weakness. Knowing his mourning for his wife had passed, I took off my widows clothes for the first time in all these years, changed, and veiled my face…as a prostitute. I positioned myself where he would have to pass.

I prayed my plan would work. I saw Judah coming. I had already determined I would not approach him. He must proposition me.

He crossed the road and walked straight to me. "What will you charge to lay with me?"

"What will you give me in return?"

"I will send a young goat back to you for payment."

Prostitutes offered goats as sacrifices at the pagan temple. So he *had* mistaken me for a prostitute, as I'd hoped. But a goat wasn't enough. I needed something personal from him. "Then leave a pledge with me to guarantee the debt will be paid."

His brow furrowed. "What kind of guarantee do you want?"

"Leave your signet, cord, and staff." As was tradition, I knew a man must have three pieces of identification with him to use when he entered into an agreement.

Judah did not hesitate. He took off the signet and cord—the one used to sign and seal all his important documents—and handed them to me, along with his signature staff.

I had relations with him. My face remained covered, and he did not recognize me.

Judah left, and when he was in the distance, I took the veil from my face, put back on my widow's clothes, and went home. I did not intend to wait there for the goat. Instead, I took his pieces of identity and went home.

The evidence I waited for had come…No showing of blood. I was pregnant with Judah's child. For me, this was the hand of God. He was the giver of life and the taker of life. This was His gift to me, but I would wait for the right time to reveal whose child I bore.

My family recognized I was pregnant.

I assured my parents as best I could. "Please do not judge me. What has happened is the will of God and soon all will be revealed, and my shame will be redeemed. Please trust me."

A few days later, I looked out to see Hirah and another man approaching.

Father opened the door. "Hirah?"

"Tamar has committed a great sin against the house of Judah and this news has traveled throughout the village. We have come to bring her to face him. There she will confess and receive her judgment from him."

Father stiffened. "Allow me the decency of bringing her to Judah. Let us say our goodbyes to our daughter in private. Please leave us and tell him what I have told you. Then we will follow you."

Father knew as well as I the "judgment" Judah would give me: burning at the stake. He had paid a bride-price for me, so I was still under his house rules and covering.

But while I saw fear on my father's face, I was at peace. For there would be judgment…

But it would not be mine.

No sooner had the door closed behind the men than my mother cried out. "Do something to save your daughter!"

I knew her anger stemmed from desperation. She could not weep, for the deities did not allow her this emotion. Father led her to kneel before the idols and beg for mercy for me.

I did not bow. These gods would not and could not save me. My God was protecting me.

I tried to comfort my parents. I kissed them. "Do not fear. For I am in the hands of the One True God. He is the God of Judah's father, Jacob, and his father Isaac before him, and of Abraham. Judah told me of His miracles and power. Do you not remember the desolation of Sodom and Gomorrah? How they paid for their evil? This same God will bring judgment or mercy on me. If I was wrong in what I did, I will be punished. But if I am found without guilt, I will be spared."

I walked out the door of my father's home to face an uncertain future. The truth that I spoke of was tucked deep in my heart…and Judah's identity was tucked in a blanket, which I carried. Father walked close. "What's in the blanket you carry, my daughter?"

"My redemption."

I was not in the wrong for I had taken what was mine, a promised right to bear children for the household of Judah. This was my inheritance too.

I might take this baby to my grave, but I would not be ashamed. I had placed my life in God's hands.

We entered the courtyard outside Judah's home. Here everyone could see him—vindicated, clearing his family name of the shame he believed I brought. The crowd pushed and fought their way for a better view.

Father squeezed my hand, and then dropped it. I looked to see Judah standing stone-faced and resolute on the steps outside his home. From his elevated position, he could see everyone and everyone could see him. Although I had always viewed him with the posture of a prince, he had changed. He now had the bearing of a judge, ready to pronounce his death sentence upon me.

There was energy in the crowd gathered and they waited for the drama to unfold. They whispered and pointed.

I moved to stand before Judah. A hush fell upon the crowd as they moved back, allowing me space.

His voice thundered over me. "Tamar, what do you say for yourself?"

Without reservation, I stooped before him and rolled out the blanket in one motion, revealing Judah's staff, signet, and chord. How they glowed in the light! I rose and looked up into his eyes. "I am pregnant by the man who owns these. See if you recognize whose seal, cord, and staff these are."

A gasp reverberated through the crowd—they knew whose property these were.

Not one sound. It was as silent as a tomb.

Judah had lost his voice...and his case.

The people would now be the judge.

The eyes transfixed on me, the one thought guilty, were now on Judah, waiting for his response.

Again—silence. No one dared utter a word.

For the judge had now become the guilty.

As the blood drained from Judah's face, I felt warmth and color come back to mine. I *was* in the right. Judah's expression proved it.

His stone face cracked and so did his voice. He spoke so all might hear: "I am the man."

His words tumbled out with determined diction. "Tamar is more righteous than I. She shall not die—she will live in my house as the esteemed mother of my child." He choked. "And he will flourish in my household as my own son. For he is bone of my bone and flesh of my flesh, my son forever, he shall be."

With this humble admission and pronouncement, applause and cheers rose from the crowd. They breathed a sigh of relief, as did I. They had come to observe the judgment of death.

They left witnesses to the redemption of life.

Judah took me into his home that very day. He sat by me. "Tamar, I have humbled and shamed you. It would not be right for me to assert the privilege of a husband. You will remain chaste in my home, but your benefits will be that of my wife. Before you and before my God, I pledge: You and your child will bear my name, I will protect and provide, I will honor and cherish you always, and I—I will be your kinsman redeemer."

I started to speak but he was not through.

"Tamar, you are the vessel through whom my God will fulfill His promise to my family. The God who delivered me, I will serve forever, and I will teach our child to walk and worship no other God. We will serve no other."

When my time came to give birth, another miracle happened! God gave us not one but two sons! Twins. Judah rushed in to see his sons, and tears welled up in his eyes. He could not speak.

I turned to face him. "Judah how mighty is your God, who would give you two sons to replace the two you buried."

We named the twins Perez and Zerah. Judah sat beside me on the bed, holding one son in each arm. "Tamar, we do not belong here. As soon our sons are strong enough, I shall take you and go back the land where I belong, to my God, my father Jacob, and my family. My father will bless them on his knee as my grandfather Isaac did for me."

This news filled me with joy. "Who knows, Judah, but that through this blessing, generations could spring forth and lead others to trust God?"

"A blessing that came through you, Tamar." He looked down at his sons. "You and this miracle have brought me back to the God of my father and birthed new life within me."

I smiled. "And I have decided, once and forever, your God shall be my God."

And so He was, forever more.

Read Tamar's Story in Genesis 38

Chapter 8

Eve

MY EYES POPPED open. Another day! Another chance to explore Eden. I clasped my hands and looked to see if the man was awake. He was not.

Yet.

I sat up, sending the zinnias I had been sleeping on flying, and hugged my knees to my chest. I rocked back and forth. What would the morning bring? Such wonders awaited us.

I looked at the man again. Still sleeping. I leaned in to stare at his closed eyes.

Nothing.

I leaned closer. Awake. Man, awake!

His mouth opened…a snore emitted.

I straightened. Bouncing my feet up and down. Oh dear, my foot reached over to nudge the man. I pulled it back and waited, holding my breath.

Another snore.

My foot did it again. But this time harder.

Success! The man's eyes opened and looked at me. A slow smile crept across his face and those strong arms stretched. He sat up. "I'm hungry." He held out his hand to pull me up. "Let's go find something to eat."

How I loved our routine of discovery. Each new dawn we explored sights and sounds here in our garden.

My eyes scanned the scarlet orchids exploding amid translucent roses. Hydrangeas matured like enormous trees in the fresh kissed dew of the morning. My nose captured the fragrance and I beheld the faultless formation of all Abba's design.

Fruit in abundance draped and hung over us. Attached to vine, tree, or bush by our Abba…for our taking. He came to visit in the cool and quiet every evening. It was our favorite part of our day. We walked and talked with Him, as we had since our beginning….

When we were with Him, He taught us so much. Yesterday He told us of babies, birthing, and what He called the cycle of all created things. He had fashioned everything to produce after its own kind. We sat at his feet as he told us "I made the earth and the heavens in one day. The earth was bare and the ground was dry for there was no water. I caused a mist to come up from the earth to water the whole surface."

So this all happened before us....

"Then I formed man from dust; breathed into his nostrils to give him life, planted the garden here in Eden, and put the man Adam here. Out of the ground, I made plants pleasing to his eye and good for his food. In the middle, I placed my tree of life and the tree of knowledge of good and evil."

I loved looking back though Abba's eyes, learning of our wondrous paradise, and the very dawning of all creation.

"Adam, when I put you, the man, in this garden, I gave you charge to tend and keep it. I commanded you to eat from any tree except the tree of knowledge of good and evil."

I loved this part. I never tired of hearing his warning to Adam.

"Remember, if you violate this command, you will die."

Adam's eyes widened and he nodded. My Adam would not defy Abba's command!

Abba talked of the greatness of the heaven and the earth, the purpose of days, and nights, all created, as we were, by His hand.

But as I listened, I knew there was nothing so great as Abba. The sound of His voice around and within me, the wisdom, and the love He shared with us...all of this, I would never forget.

Abba has left us. I cannot wait to see Him again. I looked to the sky. Today He told us how He named all the stars that branched out like trees. His shining gemstones in the sky twinkled on and off each night, just for us. And He had made the moon glow in the evening as our night light. Everything here and all that is beyond our garden, Abba made by His voice. And yet He came personally, to us, teaching, training, sharing, showing, and loving us.

How great His love!

Suddenly, I could not breathe, there was wetness in my eyes. What was this? I ran to Adam and threw my arms around him. "Look at my eyes! Listen to my breaths! What is wrong with me?"

There was a smile in his voice. "This is joy, little one."

"I do not know if I like it."

He laughed. "You will."

I reached for Adam's hand as we walked through our beautiful garden. My eyes darted back and forth, like the hummingbirds not able to decide which fragrant flower would feed them. I dropped Adam's hand to skip ahead. The cool carpet of grass caressed my toes in the lush meadow.

I motioned to Adam. I plucked a round mango, and reached for raspberries that beckoned with their brilliant blush. Each was sweet and ripe, every time. Adam put his hands on the mango and twisted. It snapped open just right. He offered me half and we sat, smiling at each other as we ate, the warm juice dribbling down our chins.

Within our reach hung profuse clusters of grapes that appeared to hang suspended in-mid air. We selected a few. The mist watered and kept them forever ripe. Just as they received water, Adam and I had everything provided for us here. I closed my eyes and was almost asleep when it happened.

Something was nudging me.

I looked down to see Adam's foot and I looked up to see his grin.

He stood. "Shall we go to the pool?"

I was on my feet almost before he finished the question.

We came upon a sleepy lion. Adam stooped to stroke his head. I knelt, placed my arms around his neck, and pulled him to me. I brushed his coarse mane with my fingers. He surrendered, dropping his head in my lap. He bestowed a kiss upon my hand with his large, rough tongue, and then the majestic lion yawned and closed his eyes, in warm satisfaction of the morning sun and my embrace. A young lamb joined us and nuzzled my hand. I lifted and cradled him and buried my face in his soft, warm fleece.

I felt strong arms come about me from behind, cradling me and my friends to his chest, Adam's deep voice whispered in my ear.

"God created them, brought them to me, one at a time, and lingered to see what name I would bestow to each."

All His creatures dwelt in harmony first with Adam and later with me. The birds worshiped, soaring heavenward, and then returned to their nests, to sing their morning serenade. Adam and I attended their concert, but God orchestrated it.

The animals and birds were Adam's first companions, long before I was his helpmate. The man was here before I was and the Creator God was here before Adam. How long was God here?

Forever.

I closed my eyes to remember the day.

The day I drew breath.

The first time I opened my eyes was to look into the face of God.

"It is not good for man to be alone."

As I took my first breath, I heard those words.

"Man?" I repeated. Startled that I had a voice and understanding.

"I caused the man Adam to fall into a deep sleep and removed a rib from which I fashioned you. Now you two will become one."

And so, He was my Creator *and* my Abba.

The second thing my eyes beheld was the man! The Maker took me to him.

"Adam, I formed you and gave you all the trees and foliage. Then I produced all the wild animals and birds of the air and placed them here for your pleasure. Still, they were not the companion you needed. With tender care, I fashioned this help-mate to complete you, as your companion."

"At last…" the man exclaimed. " This one is bone from my bone, and flesh from my flesh! She will be called woman, because she was taken from man."

My mind opened. I belonged. Together we were one.

I was home.

I snuggled next to Adam as the next words came. "Tell me everything!"

He smiled. "Our paradise abounds with living creatures, both great and small. Plants and trees without number. Springs, waterfalls, and rivers. So much to see. And, what a wonderful thing to have you here to see it with me. I did not know I needed you, but now that you are here, I cannot imagine living without you. When I think of my Creator's love, I look at you and realize how great a gift He has given me. You make paradise complete."

I gazed into his eyes. He was so big, so strong, and he cherished me!

"Tell me more."

"Now as we walk, woman, I will show you everything, just as the Father showed me. Welcome to our home."

We sat in the darkness of that first night, gazing into the star-filled sky. There were so many stars they cast a glow over us. The moon smiled down on us.

Adam slid his arm around me. "There is so much more. Tomorrow we will visit all I have spoken to you about. For now, we must sleep."

"Sleep?"

"Close your eyes and put your head on my shoulder."

Before long, I thought of nothing...and my first sleep came.

Day after day, we explored and discovered. The adventure never ended. I lost track of the days, there were so many. And then, we were back to where we started—home.

The beautiful pictures of everything we had seen filled my head. I couldn't contain my joy. It overflowed making me dance through the meadows and fields.

Today we sat on the banks of a pool. I dangled my feet in the smooth, still water. It lapped at my ankles, even as the tiny fish nibbled at my toes. I giggled, and leaned forward to see them.

Oh! There was a woman in the water! I reached out to touch her, but the moment my fingers connected with hers, the water shifted and she was gone. Then, back again! I moved an arm. She moved an arm. I leaned closer, as did she. I smiled, and so did—

It was me! I was in the water! I reached for Adam and tugged him, laughing, to lean forward. And he was there, in the water, too. Beside me! Oh! And the sky was there! A perfect frame around us. My lazy lion had followed me and stepped into the frame.

Perfect family.

I giggled. The woman in the water and I turned to hug Adam. This was my world.

Paradise.

"Pssst!"

What was this strange voice, whispering in my ear?

"Woman, oh woman."

That voice—thick and rich as if dripping with honey.

I turn to see the outline of someone. I placed my hand above my brow, blocking the brilliant sun that kept me from seeing this creature well.

"May I have a word with you?" The words rolled off his lips, drawing me, tempting me.

"Who are you?"

The creature came closer still. It looked like a man. It was a man, with splendid form. An exquisite creature! From what part of the garden did this brilliant visitor come? The tempo of his voice charmed and disarmed me. I could not resist.

"Will you stroll with me?"

Enchanted, I fell into step beside him.

"Woman, I am most eager to tell you a secret you MUST know."

"What secret?"

"Of all the creatures in this paradise, you are by far the most perfect."

Perfect. Yes, I am perfect.

"But something is missing."

"No, you are wrong. Abba has given me everything."

"Woman…You…Have no…idea!"

His voice grasped me.

"Too bad your Abba put such restrictions on you."

"I have no restrictions…except—"

I looked away from him, to the path ahead. "Oh no! What's this?"

"This…My Lady, is the doorway…to your freedom!"

"I cannot be here. I must go! Abba said…"

"But, you have every right to be here. For this is your paradise, is it not?"

My heart raced but I could not bring myself to flee. "But that is THE tree, I cannot eat of it!"

"Oh, did God really say, 'You must not eat from any tree in the garden?'"

"We may eat from all the trees in the garden—but God told Adam, 'You must not eat of the tree in the middle of the garden, and you must not touch it, or you will die.'"

He laughed. "You will not die! For God knows that when you eat from it your eyes will be opened. When you partake of it, and only then…you will be like God, knowing all good and evil."

All good and evil? "There is more?" *Had Abba not told me everything?*

"Oh yes, there is much, much more and you can have it all! You should have it all, should you not?" I looked straight into the dazzling forbidden tree, breathless and speechless. Desire begged as bittersweet assent washed over me. I reached out to touch. The very feel of the fruit drew me.

But…the touch was not enough. I *had* to taste.

I bit.

Delicious!

"Woman!"

The fruit clutched in my hand, I turned to see Adam.

"Adam, oh Adam! Look at me! I did not die—nor will you. It was *not* the truth!"

Adam stared at me. For the first time since I first opened my eyes, I did not know what he was thinking. There was something between us. I did not like it. I wanted him with me but there was only one way….

I handed him the fruit. Sweet juice trickled on his hand. He put it to his lips.

And then he ate.

We were still alive. We had not died. The creature was correct—I looked to see he had departed. Yet in the distance, I heard his dark laugh echoing in my ears, and something washed though me...something heavy, something terrible.

Shame.

I exhaled. I turned to Adam. I needed him to comfort me. But I stopped, drew back. He was naked! His face grew scarlet but the color drained from mine. I covered myself with my arms.

I looked at the fig tree—its leaves were the largest in the garden. I grabbed them, jerked them from the tree. With their stems, I wove them together, put one on me, and handed one to Adam. These would cover us.

But they would not hide us, not from Abba.

What if God found us this way, in our humiliation? We crouched among the brushwood and flora. A voice cried out. It was mine. "Why did I judge God? Why did I listen to the creature?"

Amazing truth now stunned me—I *was* already perfect.

But no more.

The tempter was correct in one way: I saw evil and iniquity for the first time, and it was mine.

The cool breezes blew. We heard the Lord God walking in the garden as He did every evening. For the first time, I did not run to welcome Him. Instead, I crouched lower.

"Adam, where are you?"

The man beside me spoke and I did not recognize his voice. The music was gone, the joy gone, and in their place, something I have never heard before.

Fear.

"Abba, I heard you walking in the garden, so I hid. I was afraid because I was naked."

"Who told you that you were naked?"

Was this Abba's voice? Why did it sound so—distant?

"Have you eaten the fruit of the tree from which I commanded you not to eat?"

The man beside me now sank deeper into the brush. "It was the woman you gave me. She offered me the fruit and I ate."

Heat welled within me. He was blaming me? Or was he blaming Abba?

What had happened to my protector?

I looked to God, ready to defend myself and His eyes met mine.

"Woman, what have you done?"

Now it was my turn to crouch deeper. "The serpent seduced me. That is why I ate."

The dark laughter was there again. I looked up to see the tempter peering out from behind a tree. But like us, he could not hide from Abba.

The Creator turned to face him and now His voice was that of a judge.

"Because you have done this, you are cursed more than all animals, domestic and wild. You will crawl on your belly, groveling in the dust as long as you live. And I will cause hostility between you and the woman, and between your offspring and her offspring. He will strike your head, and you will strike his heel."

The serpent slumped and writhed on the ground, his very form changing into a reptile-like creature. His tongue darted in and out like a jagged fork. He lost his ability to walk and talk and now made naught but a hissing sound. Scales covered his body. Reduced to a detestable figure, his very appearance gave me chills. I watched as he slithered out of the garden on his belly.

And now it was my turn. "Woman." The Creator looked into my tear-filled eyes. "I will multiply the pain of your childbearing, and you'll give birth to your young in pain. And you will desire to control your husband, but he will rule over you."

But no, this was too much. Why did the Creator not restore me? I did not want this. I never wanted this.

And yet—I ate.

He turned to the man.

"Because you listened to your wife and ate from the tree I forbade you, the very ground is cursed because of you. Getting food from the ground will be as painful as having babies will be for your wife; you'll be working in pain all your life long. The ground will sprout thorns and weeds, you'll get food the hard way, planting, tilling, and harvesting. You will sweat in the fields from dawn to dusk, until you return to that ground yourself, dead and buried—you started out as dirt, you'll end up dirt."

Adam dropped his head into the cradle of his hands.

So this was guilt....

In disobeying our Creator, we had discovered yet another new thing.

Sin.

The Creator gave us time to sit with our reality, but He did not forsake us. He did something so beautiful after we confessed. He fashioned more permanent coverings of 'coats of skin' to clothe us. For Adam, He created a handsome leather shroud and for me, a fur covering. I looked down to stroke the fur and my hand stilled.

My lion.

It was my lion.

He had died to cover my sin.

God's perfect, beloved, and innocent animal's blood spilled on the ground for the first time. A symbol of His love for us, the first to be disobedient, first punished...and yet still precious to Him.

Were we banished forever? The death we experienced that day was both physical and spiritual separation from our Creator. And the reality of that loss was worse than physical death. Absence from my Father broke my heart.

As darkness settled over paradise, darkness settled over me. Strange and foreboding. I could not understand this feeling of separation. The man and I would leave Eden—never to return.

And that's when I knew.

This was the death.

The Creator had not lied.

God placed a barrier between our world and the garden. No human would ever enter that paradise again. It was forever sealed.

A deep realization overcame me. I was homeless.

"Oh Adam, what have we done?"

He took me in his strong arms and buried his face in my hair. "I am so sorry. I should have protected you. I promise never to fail you again. Whatever we face—fear, sorrow, danger, or pain, I will stand beside you and we shall face life, as it should be. Together."

I wept.

He cupped my face in his hands. "You are the mother of all mankind and as a new dawn springs forth, I will call you Eve."

In this new world, I had a companion I had never known before.

Fear.

In Eden, we had not needed the safety of a shelter but here, outside, there was danger everywhere.

We walked to a forest plain, I fought off bugs that buzzed in my face and bit my skin. Each new step brought new pain. Stickers on the ground pierced my feet and we had to climb over tree trunks in the way. In Eden, we walked for days and never grew weary, but now…our energy waned and we grew tired.

Adam held me as we lay down on the grass. It provided our bed that first night. We could not find a bed of zinnias. I pushed closer. "Why am I shivering?"

"It is cold. We will need to cover with foliage for warmth."

I closed my eyes trying to find the sweet sleep that had come so easily but could not because of the screams and cries in the darkness.

I reached for Adam's hand. "What's happening?"

"There are beasts of prey in this place, roaming the forest, looking for food. They do not eat grass and berries but look for flesh to eat. The larger animals have dominion here."

"How could this be? The animals are not our friends?"

"No. Here they roam wild and untamed. Their spirit no longer abides with man. We are strangers to them as they are to us."

I pressed my face against his chest and my tears anointed his skin. "How do you know these terrible things?"

His voice was raw, choked. "The Creator has given me this knowledge."

So, the serpent had been right. We had gained knowledge.

And it was death to us.

The dawn of our first day alone, Adam rose and gathered rocks, branches, and vines. I crept close and watched him use these things to make…what?

"What are you making?"

He pointed to one group of items. "These are tools to till the ground."

I looked at the other items. "And those?"

His voice lowered. "Those are weapons. For our safety. The Creator told me we would need them."

The Creator? "He was here?"

Adams' forehead creased. "Yes…but not like before. I did not see him. But I heard him." He touched a hand to his chest. "In here."

Over the next few days, I saw Adam had learned much from his time with the Creator. Now aware of our first need, Adam built a fine shelter.

Once more, I had a home.

The days passed much as they had in Eden. But here we faced the elements of wind, sun, and cold. Not all the fruits were ripe. We had to wander further to find them. I reached to pick a rose. Adam grabbed my hand. "Be careful…of the thorns."

I drew back. "My beautiful roses have thorns?"

"The berries have briars and you must use caution picking them for they will tear your hands and arms."

It wasn't just the world around us that changed. Our very bodies were changing. One day, I found blood on my bed when I arose in the morning. And there was pain—deep, wrenching cramping in my abdomen.

I cried out for Adam. He came running, and put his arms around me where I curled on my bed.

"Adam! It hurts! I'm bleeding! I'm dying!"

But even as the words left my lips, understanding came. This was as the Creator had foretold. This was part of the cycle of life.

Outside of the garden.

I buried my face in Adam's shoulder. "Does everything now bring pain?"

He did not answer.

He did not need to.

Each day, I prepared food, brought water, and tended the fire. We soon understood about living by the sweat of our brow.

Through Adam's hard work, we survived. He tilled, planted, weeded, and harvested our garden. There was a never-ending need of firewood. So much energy and strength required just to make it through a day.

Adam gathered herds of livestock, sheep, goats, and cattle. We became farmers, growing fields of vegetables and fruit orchards. As days and months passed, Adams daily routine brought him satisfaction in providing for us. He enjoyed seeing new life from his livestock, and watching seeds sprout in his garden. He loved the provisions they brought.

When we left Eden, I was sure our lives were over. But even here, away from perfection, we were able to keep going. The Creator was still with us. Not as before, but we knew He still watched over and protected us.

With each new day, I vowed to obey the Creator. He knew what was best for me. He encouraged me even now that I was not perfect. And, I was comforted by that.

I had learned my lesson. I would protect my relationship with my husband and my Creator Father. I wanted to make wise choices, to seek Adam's and the Creator's counsel, but something deep within made this very desire a struggle.

I asked the Creator what was happening and He opened my understanding. My disobedience had opened a door no man could close, and through it, sin forever bonded to the nature of man.

The weight of this responsibility would have been unbearable if I had not had the memory of God's mercy in the garden—and the evidence of His continued mercy here.

With time and The Creator's love, my joy returned. One morning He whispered to me that I had conceived and would bear a child in our image, Adam's and mine.

Four months passed, and then I felt it.

A flutter. In my abdomen. My heart leapt as the Creator told me, "This is your child."

My stomach grew after that, and more sensations came.

A pushing from within: "Your child stretches."

A poke just below my ribcage: "Your child's fist, pushing against you."

A protrusion in my belly: "This is your child's heel."

With each new discovery, I ran to Adam and grabbed his hand, bringing it to my growing belly. And his smile grew even broader.

After another four months of watching my body change shape, I wanted this process to be over! How long would this take? Was I to be like this forever? My lower back ached and my feet swelled. Would my stomach explode if it grew more?

One morning I awoke to intense pain. I cried out to Adam. The agony came in waves, letting up for a moment, and then intensifying even more. That was when I remembered: "I'll multiply your pains in childbirth…."

I called on the Creator, begging Him to end the torture. I gripped Adam's hand and panted out a cry: "I am being torn apart from the inside!"

And then, when the pain was at its worst, Adam yelled to me, "You must push, Eve. Push!"

"I cannot!"

"You must! Or the child will die."

I did not ask how he knew this. The Creator had told him. And so I pushed. Screaming. Weeping. And pushed again. And again. And…

Our child was born!

Relief swept me, and now my tears were not of pain, but joy. The most intense joy I had ever felt. Adam's face glowed as he gazed down at our child.

"You have given me a son, Eve." He laid the babe on my stomach. "Our son. You are the mother of all mankind."

Without knowing why I was doing so, I wrapped the babe and held him to my breast. He suckled, and I knew yet another new joy. I had given life. I was giving life even now. This was our miracle. A gift from the Creator.

Adam and I were created as adults, but our child was born tiny and helpless. He needed us. Just as we needed the Creator. We would watch our child grow and become like us.

"What will you call him Eve?"

The name was there. "He is Cain."

Motherhood was sweet. I sensed how much the Creator God loved us, His children.

Beyond life itself.

My love bonded me to Cain in an indescribable way. So this was family....

My baby learned to pull up, crawl, and walk, commanding my full attention. Cries of, "Me, me, me," and "I want, I want...and no, no, no" filled our home. I rushed to please him.

Before long, I conceived again. The mystery of that first birth was gone but the pain was not. It would be present every time.

My reminder.

I gave birth to our second child, and Adam laid him on my chest. "We have another son." We named him Abel.

As time passed, something terrible happened. Cain started picking on the baby and was mean to him. I had to watch to keep Abel safe. I scolded Cain but to no avail. I wanted to weep, because my children were disobedient, just as Adam and I had been.

That's when I understood the awful truth. In my disobedience to the Creator, I passed on a sinful nature to my children! They would have to experience their own relationship with the Creator. As Adam and I had.

I wanted to shelter them from the consequences of life, of their own choices. To make them obey the rules and guidelines for living. But I could not.

Cain grew up to be a planter and enjoyed the gardens and orchards, while Abel became a herdsman. Abel was naturally sweet and loving, drawn to his Creator but Cain acted out of obligation and resentment.

Because of my sin, would harboring hate and being jealous never cease to stalk humanity? Man against God, Satan against man, and brother against brother?

Adam came to me. He was troubled. "I watched Cain during his first harvest and told him that the first fruits of his harvest go to the Lord God. Cain resisted. 'But it's mine! I made it!'"

"The Creator made it."

"He did not till the ground, or plant the seed! He did not tote the water and care for the plants! I did it."

One day Cain returned home and I knew something devastating had taken place. He looked around our home, as though mad, and then ran out again. I followed him, and that's when I overheard the Creator calling to Cain, asking about Abel. "Where is your brother Abel?"

He lied. "I don't know. Am I my brother's keeper?"

He had murdered my Abel. I came to Adam sobbing. This was the first time I saw Adam cry. We laid face down beside our garden, grieving until long after the sun had set. Adam rose. "This is where we will bury him."

Would we ever be healed from this loss? I wept for all I brought to my sons, and the sons after them, and the sons after them. God had destined all my generations to live in perfection, but by my act of disobedience, I had now destined them to struggle with jealousy and hatred.

And so much more.

So much worse.

I lost both my sons that day. I mourned at losing one son through physical death and the other by separation. Cain had moved far away to the land of Nod. Such sorrow and heartache! The Creator had forgiven me, but forgiveness did not stop the consequences of my wrong choices.

Losing two treasures of my heart, my children, devastated me. Now Adam and I were alone again. Every day, every action—working in the fields, preparing food, cooking—it all reminded me of my loss.

In time, God opened doors through which my healing began. I planted a flower garden near the place where we buried Abel. Each day I came to care for the flowers, I sat and communed with the Creator. Slowly, I enjoyed time outside again in His creation. I learned to depend on Him more every day. I asked Him to fill the void that haunted me. He blessed me with His love and care.

I will never forget the day I knew. My relationship with Him was better after the fall than ever before. How could this be?

Because I now understood the depth of His love. In the garden, I was a child, spending time with Abba without realizing how precious it all was. Now, I knew my sin and what it had cost me. Cost us all. And yet…

He loved me.

In the face of my sin, His love was more wondrous than ever before.

One day He whispered. "Whose child are you?"

"I am Yours."

And I was. Forever.

In time, God gave me another son, Seth. Joy returned. I vowed to do things the right way this time. Adam and I dedicated him to the Creator and asked for His help as we raised him.

Receiving another chance at parenting was the best gift God gave us besides His forgiveness. One day the wonder at this gift overflowed, and I told Adam, "I have gotten a man from the Lord."

As I spoke the word Lord, I knew. This was another name for the Creator. He was my Creator and my Lord.

Seth produced a godly generation and when his son Enosh became a father, my heart wondered at hearing men call upon the name of the Lord!

There would never be another Eden. The earth was cursed through my disobedience. I didn't plan to sin, but I didn't plan not to. And yet, for all that, the Creator was with us. He drew my family, generation after generation, to Him. He restored me. He restored us all, when we turned to Him.

I experienced the beauty of belonging—even in my sin, shame, and imperfection. I was no longer perfect, but…I was His. And that was enough.

The Creator showed me that paradise is still there. What's more, it awaits us! But the path to this home lies through the doorway of death. I once walked and talked with God, in person, every day. Although I lost that privilege, when I die, I will go to Him again. And we will walk and talk.

In His paradise.

A paradise I will never, ever leave.

Read Eve's story in Genesis 2-4

Glossary of Terms Used

Abba: A name used in the Bible to address God.

Adonai: A name used in Judaism instead of the unspeakable name of God

Adullam: A Canaanite city mentioned in the Bible in Gen. 38:1, South of Jerusalem and near the Dead Sea.

Altar: A place of prayer, slaughter, or sacrifice. In the Hebrew Bible, they were typically made of earth or unwrought stone. Abraham, Isaac, and Jacob erected altars.

Bedouin: A predominantly desert-dwelling Arabian ethnic group traditionally divided into tribes or clans.

Bethel: A town about 10 miles north of Jerusalem. It was here that Abraham encamped in this beautiful pastureland. It received the name of Bethel—House of God, because of Jacob's dream.

Bride-price: An amount of money, property, or wealth paid by the groom or his family to the parents of a woman upon the marriage of their daughter to the groom.

Canaan/Canaanite: A historical/Biblical region and people in the present-day Gaza Strip, Israel, West Bank, and Lebanon.

Concubine: A woman who cohabits with a man to whom she is not legally married, especially one regarded as socially or sexually subservient. Among polygamous peoples, a secondary wife, usually of inferior rank.

Covenant: An agreement, usually formal, between two or more persons to do or not do something specified.

Dead Sea: Also called the Salt Sea is a salt lake bordering Jordan to the east and Israel and the West Bank to the west. It is earth's lowest elevation on land.

Deities: A deity is a being, object, or image, thought to have superhuman powers or qualities.

Dowry: A dowry is the money, goods, or estate that a woman brings to the marriage. It contrasts with bride-price, which is paid by the groom or his family to the bride's parents, and dower, which is property given to the bride herself by the groom at the time of marriage. Dowry is an ancient custom and still expected in some parts of the world, mainly South Asia.

Eden: The Garden of Eden is the biblical garden of God, described most notably in the Book of Genesis 2-3, but also mentioned, directly or indirectly, in Ezekiel, Isaiah, and elsewhere in the Old Testament.

Edom: A Semitic inhabited historical region of the Southern Levant located south of Judea and the Dead Sea. It is mentioned in biblical records as a 1st millennium BCE Iron Age kingdom of Edom. The name Edom means red in Hebrew, and was given to Esau once he ate the red pottage, which the Bible used in irony at the fact he was born *red all over.*

Edomites: The Holy Bible and The Torah describe the Edomites as descendants of Esau, the eldest son of Isaac and Rebekah.

Elohim: A Hebrew word for God.

En Gedi: An oasis in Israel, located west of the Dead Sea, near Masada and the caves of Qumran.

Euphrates: The longest and one of the most historically important rivers of Western Asia. Together with the Tigris, it is one of the two defining rivers of Mesopotamia.

GENERATIONAL SIN: Generational sins, curses, and patterns are attitudes, actions, beliefs, behaviors, and/or habits inherited from our ancestors.

GODS: A set of all the gods of a particular polytheistic religion or mythology.

HARAN: Ancient city of Mesopotamia, now in SE Asian Turkey. It was an important center frequently mentioned in the Bible and home of Abraham's family after leaving Ur. Laban, Rebekah, Leah, and Rachel lived there.

HEBRON: A town in the mountains of Judah and between Beersheba and Jerusalem, about 20 miles from each. Among those who lived there were the Canaanites, Abraham and Sarah, Hagar and Ishmael, Isaac and Rebekah, Jacob and Leah. David made it his royal residence. All the Matriarchs and Patriarchs were buried there except Rachel who was buried near Bethlehem.

HITTITE: The children of Heth are a people mentioned in the Hebrew Bible in Book of Genesis as second of the twelve Canaanite nations.

IDOL: An image or other material object representing a deity of worship or any person or thing regarded with blind admiration, adoration, or devotion.

MEMPHIS: City and capital of ancient Egypt. Located south of the Nile River delta, on the west bank of the river, and about 15 miles south of modern Cairo. Home to the famous pyramids of Egypt.

MESOPOTAMIA: Modern-day Iraq. The name means 'Between Waters' (the Tigris and Euphrates rivers.) Often dubbed as the cradle of civilization.

MIKVAH: (Hebrew) A ritual purification and cleansing bath that Orthodox Jews take on certain occasions (as before Sabbath or after menstruation) a ritual bath used by women for purification after emerging from the state of Niddah.

MYRRH: A fragrant gum resin obtained from certain trees and used, especially in the Near East, in perfumery, medicines, and incense.

NEGEV: A desert region of southern Israel. The region's largest city and administrative capital is Beersheba in the north and Gulf of Aqaba in the southern end.

NIDDAH: A Hebrew term describing a woman during menstruation, or a woman who has not yet completed the requirement of immersion in a mikvah (ritual bath).

PAPYRUS: A material prepared in ancient Egypt from the pithy stem of a water plant, used throughout the ancient Mediterranean world for writing or painting on. Also for making rope, sandals, and boats.

PARAN: A wilderness situated in the eastern central region of the Sinai Peninsula, with the Gulf of Aqabah as its eastern border. It was to this wilderness that Hagar and Ishmael went after their expulsion from Abraham's household.

PATRIARCH: In Judaism, patriarch refers to the three patriarchs Abraham, Isaac, and Jacob, who are the forefathers of Israel. It may also refer to the 12 sons of Jacob.

PHILISTINE: A member of a non- Semitic people of southern Palestine in ancient times, who came into conflict with the Israelites during the 12th and 11th centuries BC.

PROPHETS: Hebrew Bible prophets warned the Israelites to repent of their sins and idolatries, with the threat of punishment or reward. They were God's voice to the nations. Nathan rebuked David for his sin against Bathsheba.

SEIR: A mountainous region occupied by the Edomites, extending along the eastern side of the Arabia from the south-eastern extremity of the Dead Sea to near the Aqabah, or the eastern branch of the Red Sea.

SHECHEM: The Canaanite city of ancient Palestine and the first capital of the Kingdom of Israel.

Shofar: A Jewish instrument most often made from a ram's horn, though it can also be made from the horn of a sheep or goat. It makes a trumpet-like sound.

Sodom and Gomorrah: Ancient cities near the Dead Sea. Divine judgment by Yahweh was passed upon Sodom and Gomorrah along with two other neighboring cities that were completely consumed by fire and brimstone.

Supplanter: One who usurps by intrigue or underhanded tactics.

Temple Prostitutes: High places had chambers for sacred prostitution by male prostitutes and sacred harlots.

The Thirty: David had thirty top warrior men he depended upon for everything. As they died or were killed, they were replaced by others who had shown valor, integrity, and strength.

Ur: A major city, and later the capital of Mesopotamia. Its location near the sea made it a center of commerce and trade routes. Between 2030-1980 BC Ur was the world's largest city.

Wedding Tent: According to Jewish wedding customs, the bride and groom were hidden away for a week before making their first public appearance as man and wife since they typically would not have spent any time alone together before their wedding.

Yahweh: A name of God, expanded from the four letters YHWH that form the name of God in Hebrew.

Books Referenced

A LINEAGE OF GRACE: Francine Rivers

A WOMAN'S GUIDE TO BREAKING BONDAGES: Quin Sherrer & Ruthanne Garlock

ALL THE WOMEN OF THE BIBLE: Herbert Lockyer

ALL THE WOMEN OF THE BIBLE: M.L. del Mastro

BAD GIRLS OF THE BIBLE: Liz Curtis Higgs

BATHSHEBA: Jill Eileen Smith

DESPERATE WOMEN OF THE BIBLE: Jo Kadlecek

ERDMAN'S HANDBOOK TO THE BIBLE: Alexander

HAVAH THE STORY OF EVE: Tosca Lee

HOLY BIBLE: King James, New King James, New Living, The Message, and NIV

LOST WOMEN OF THE BIBLE: Carolyn Custis James

REALLY BAD GIRLS OF THE BIBLE: Liz Curtis Higgs

REDEEMING LOVE: Francine Rivers

SLIGHTLY BAD GIRLS OF THE BIBLE: Liz Curtis Higgs

THE ONE YEAR WOMEN OF THE BIBLE: Dianne Neal Matthews

TWELVE EXTRAORDINARY WOMEN: John MacArthur

TWELVE APOSTOLIC WOMEN: Joanne Turpin

UNASHAMED: Francine Rivers

UNVEILED: Francine Rivers

WOMEN AT THE TIME OF THE BIBLE: Miriam Feinberg Vamosh

About the Author

Carol Cook understands women's issues. As a philanthropist in Arizona, she has served on prestigious boards for women, helping raise funds for many charities. Her mission is to help women and children in crisis while raising awareness by educating others to important needs in her community.

Carol has mentored young women for many years and takes personal interest in their life stories, encouraging them to write about their journeys. She writes and leads Bible Studies and in particular, stories of the women of the Bible, in the first person, showing how their stories are not unlike issues we still face today, some 6000 years later. She invites us into these lives so real and current, it seems like today's story.

She continues to write Bible women's stories and is currently writing another book of eight Old Testament women and later will add eight Bible Women from the New Testament to complete her "Truth be Told Trilogy."

Carol lives in Paradise Valley, Arizona and is married to Jim, her husband of 48 years. They have three adult children and ten grandchildren. She loves creative writing, music, travel, research, and decorating.